THE GINGER FLIC CASEBOOK

DUARTE FIGUEIRA

© Copyright Duarte Figueira 2021

All Rights Reserved

ISBN 978-1-7398673-1-7

Published by Dewey Press
duartf@icloud.com

A CIP catalogue record for this title is available from the British Library.

Cover design Jo Faulkner

Typesetting by Coinlea Services
www.coinlea.co.uk

Acknowledgements

I am deeply grateful to the Writers of Whitstable (WoW) for their generous advice and support. I must also give my heartfelt thanks to Lin White of Coinlea Word Services for being such a great editor and advisor on this book and to Jo Faulkner for her beautiful cover design. And finally of course, to Felicia and Ross for just being themselves.

To Denise

Contents

Murderous Beginnings

I HEARD THE KINCAIDS GUN BEN DOWN ON A QUIET SUNDAY morning in Stoke Newington when he went out to get the papers. My head jerked up in our postage stamp garden when I heard the bullets flying. Some primal instinct told me it was him and I felt at that moment as if my throat had been slit.
I crept out to see the scene after the Forensics Team had left, but when I saw the bloody mess in the doorway to which the bullets had pinned him, I fell to pieces.

So I already knew he was dead when Rick and Winslow came to pick up his laptop and papers the next morning. I was lying on the sofa, totally out of it with grief. Rick was Ben's guvnor and Winslow his partner before he'd gone undercover. They stroked me and forced me to eat and drink something. They left me in the kitchen while they gathered up Ben's stuff, but they forgot how good a cat's hearing is when they spoke in the lounge.

'He said he was getting close to the Kincaids,' said Winslow.

'Yea, too close,' said Rick.

'No doubt, no doubt,' Winslow answered.

He was almost crying.

They both looked over at me as they were getting ready to leave.

'What about Ginger Flic?' Rick asked.

'She needs looking after. I'll ring Ben's sister Grace, see if she can stay with her in Whitstable.'

So that's how I got here, to Whelkville as I like to call it, four months ago, just before lockdown. Grace drove me down and I decided to stay for just as long as I needed. Someday, I'll thank her and be on my way. But just now Grace and I still need each other to get over Ben's murder. As if we ever will.

You'll want to know something about me. Well, its Flic, short for Felicia. And no one says I'm beautiful. My head's too big, my legs too short and my body barrel-shaped and inelegant. I've been round the block a thousand times and it's starting to show on the bodywork. My best feature is my fur. I'm not really ginger – I'm tri-colour calico, that's ginger with black and white, which is good for keeping out of sight in my line of work. But the name Ben gave me stuck. Apart from all that, I'm built for what I do, which is now to be the scourge of the criminal fraternity here in Whelkville. And before I leave, there will need to be payback for the Kincaids when our paths finally cross.

Meanwhile, I'm going to get ready by raising a whirlwind against crime in this dirty little seaside town. I'll need help, of course, but just being with Ben taught me everything he knew and I've watched every TV procedural ever made, sitting next to him on that old sofa in his basement flat. You see, he was a straight-as-a-die Detective Inspector in the Met. So

I've already got game and it's only going to get stronger and stronger, until I'm ready for the final showdown.

Before you scoff, remember that this is where the Krays brought their victims to torture and dispose of in the local woods. People only talk about them knee-capping their rivals in Clapton and burying them in Epping Forest. But you slip into the mean alleys of this town, or step into the pubs and antique shops, and you can still hear the East End vowels of all the guys who went legit in the 80s – the bright ones who got away. We could walk together around these streets and I could point out the big house of every ex-villain who preferred to drink proper beer and not die of skin cancer on the Costa Brava. And his neighbour and golfing buddy, the retired bent copper who always looked the other way. It's all as cosy as my favourite blanket. Everybody knows it and everyone keeps it quiet but there's crime in the local DNA. You can see it when their kids follow them into the family business.

There were always villains here. Highwaymen kept standing reservations in the inns on the London Road and smugglers docked their ships in the harbour on moonless nights. Now their successors bring in modern slaves in inflatables and keep up their end of drug county lines. It's not all bijou oyster eateries, art shacks and shabby-chic beach huts.

How do I know all this stuff and why do I care, you ask. After all, for most of my life I was a city girl living with Ben in North London. Because Ben knew this place, as he was raised here and his sis Grace still lives in Whitstable. And she didn't mind me coming down with him when he took his infrequent leave. Bring Ginger Flic down, I'd hear her say over the phone, she's a lot of fun. And I loved her for it.

Talking of needing help, I nearly forgot the third occupant of our unhappy home. That's Ross, who shared the house with Grace when I arrived. He's a tabby, he's smart, pretty and a marshmallow. Say boo to him and he'll hide for days, but he has his uses. He knows the neighbourhood and he's soft enough to see things I miss. And get this, he's a male who reads without moving his mouth. Sometimes, I can use a little muscle and a lookout, even a flaky one. And the final plus is that he's scared to death of me.

One night shortly after arrival I sat upstairs on the sofa in my room watching the sunset flaring across the sea, dripping its blood-red light over the Isle of Sheppey. Grace's house is up high on the hill and the town was spread below me like a shabbily patched quilt. I could look west across the golf course towards Seasalter and east to Tankerton slopes, with Whelkville the meat in the sandwich. I thought to myself that somewhere down that hill there would be a crime that night. It could be a murder in some rich Londoner's weekend pad, involving coke and sex toys, or it could be an allotment shed break-in involving seed packets and stained tea mugs. It didn't matter, I told myself. I'm going to clean up this dirty slice of paradise.

For you, Ben.

1

The Neighbourly Gazebo Murder

I T DIDN'T TAKE LONG FOR TROUBLE TO ARRIVE IN WHELKVILLE. The morning after my epiphany the front doorbell rang at about 9.30am. Grace's doorway and entrance is made of reinforced glass, so I could see a woman outside resting against a police car. She was about thirty-five, cropped blond hair with a pair of Ray Bans perched on her crown. Her piercing blue eyes contrasted strongly with the bloodshot whites. Her slim frame fitted well into a crumpled grey suit and her collar was undone and tieless. She looked like she'd been up all night drinking and fighting and I liked her immediately. A young constable stood beside her, dark-haired and anonymous in his blues, a downcast, embarrassed look on his face at the state of her. Hecate, I thought, don't they toughen them up at Hendon anymore?

Grace came to the door and picked me up before opening it. I wrestled a little in her arms, just out of habit. Ross scurried for the back cat flap.

'Good morning, officers. How can I help you?' she said.

The plainclothes policewoman detached herself slowly

and wearily from the car panelling. She flashed her ID open for a second. Even at this distance she didn't smell good.

'Good morning, Ms Johns. I'm DI Jane Austenson, Kent CID. This is Constable Alf Tennyson. We are looking into an incident on your road,' she said. 'Is there somewhere we can talk and remain distanced?'

Austenson and Tennyson. Whoever put these two together didn't lack a sense of humour.

They came through the back gate and sat down next to each other at the garden table. Grace offered them coffee, glancing at Austenson, who looked distinctly uncomfortable with the sunlight in her eyes. She solved that problem by lowering her shades and looking down at a small notebook she'd taken out of her inside jacket pocket. Very cool.

Then they started with the questions. Ross and I sat on the garden tiles listening. I was rapt – was this really happening? My first Whelkville investigation! Ross seemed less excited. He licked his paws and then his arse. True to form.

'You run the local Neighbourhood Watch, don't you, Ms Johns?' said Austenson.

'Grace, please. That's right.'

'So you will know Ms Jo Crawford at number 13, Grace?'

'I see her occasionally, but she's not very active in the NHW. She's some sort of travelling academic, isn't she?' Grace answered.

'And a property developer,' said Tennyson.

'Well, I know she has developed her own house – doubled it in size. Have you spoken to Bill Davis, the residents' association chair? He and his wife Lisbet are her neighbours at number 15.'

'We've spoken to most residents, but now I'm speaking to

you,' said Austenson.

There was an unfriendly edge to the voice which made Grace frown and sit up straighter. Classic nice cop, bad cop, I thought.

'We found Ms Crawford dead this morning. She was lying on the pedestal steps of her gazebo. We are treating her death as suspicious,' said Austenson.

Grace went pale, though I felt all my Xmases had come at once, to my shame. Or not.

Then young Tennyson spoke.

'Did you know that Ms Crawford had built a gazebo at the end of her garden?'

'Yes, for naked sunbathing, she told me. And it's rather large, isn't it – we called it the temple of Jo. Something of a street scandal,' said Grace.

'Really?'

'Jo didn't like to be overlooked so she built it down the garden facing east, with high latticing installed on both fences behind her so she could not be overlooked from the other houses.'

'So why the furore?' asked Austenson.

'Her neighbours on both sides objected to the high lattice fences. Lisbet is a prize-winning landscape gardener, known for her precise geometric paradigm-shifting designs. She said it obscured the light in her show-garden. But that was not the only cause of the excitement.'

'What was?' asked Austenson.

'Jo also butchered the fruit trees at the end of her garden to get more sun earlier. The garden slopes down and that meant she could see the graveyard and church beyond the footpath that runs behind the gardens. There's been a few funeral parties who have complained about getting a morning eyeful. I'm sure the vicar will confirm it.'

'Thanks, we will check that out. What is his name?'

'Her. Reverend Etty James.'

Austenson smiled as she noted the name down.

'Did you know Ms Crawford had recently installed a jacuzzi and hot tub next to the gazebo?' said Tennyson.

'No – good God.'

'Or that she used it at night and some of the neighbours had complained about the noise disturbance when she had gentleman guests?'

'That sounds like Jo.'

The detective and constable looked at one another.

'You don't sound too concerned about her death, Ms Johns, if you don't mind me saying,' said Austenson.

Grace looked at Austenson and then Tennyson.

'Of course I am. But she was a rather inconsiderate neighbour and there won't be wailing in the streets.'

'Do you know who she was concerned was overlooking her?' asked Austenson.

'Well, her neighbours are Bill and Lisbet, and Carl Popper at number 11. But I can't see either man as peeping Toms myself.'

'What do you know about Mr Popper?' said Austenson.

'He's a sensitive soul. Jo's Rottweiler, Tyson, did eat his cat Rosie last year. Which reminds me, where was Tyson?'

I'd been asking myself that for five minutes. But Austenson was not to be deflected.

'We'll come to that. Anyone else who might have a grudge against her?'

'Well, her ex-husband, Jonny, I suppose. Jonny Miro. She

bragged that she had cleaned him out during the divorce. Got the house and used the settlement to fund the extension and this gazebo. And the jacuzzi, hot tub and God knows what else.'

Austenson and Tennyson looked at each other and got up to leave before uttering the rote words.

'Thank you, Ms Johns. You've been very helpful.'

Grace and I walked them to the door, or rather Grace carried me. Austenson held Grace's gaze a second longer than needed when they said goodbye. Hallo, I thought. Grace finally asked the question that I'd been itching to ask throughout.

'Why do you really think that Jo's death is suspicious?'

Austenson sighed.

'Tyson was found poisoned, possibly accidentally, at the end of the garden, near the trees.'

I was already wrestling to get out of Grace's arms. I wanted to do my own CSI on the scene asap. Austenson stroked my head.

'Feisty little thing, isn't she?'

As the cop car pulled away from the drive Grace put me down and looked me in the eye.

'You liked our dishy detective, didn't you?' she said.

I looked right back at her. Not as much as you, I thought.

◆

One of the advantages of being a domestic pet is that you are rarely noticed. With Tyson out of the picture there was nothing to keep me out of Jo's garden. No time like the present. Ignoring his squeaking protests, I told Ross to follow me at a discreet distance as we balanced along the panel fencing that acts as our highway behind the houses on White Horse Road.

We dropped into the rear of Jo's garden in the heat of the midday sun and sought shade under her drastically pruned fruit trees. Ahead, we could see police incident marker tape stretched between planted poles, restricting access to a large part of the garden. That included the area around the monstrous gazebo which rose in concrete steps to a floor height of about four feet above the surrounding lawn. At the top, six concrete Ionian pillars held up a meshed wooden ceiling frame under which sagged the gold and purple cotton sunshades. The over-sized jacuzzi and heat tub combo sat like a squat green flying saucer on the lawn a few yards away. Never mind the murder, the taste bypass on show was criminal all by itself.

A small incident tent set at an awkward angle covered the steps of the gazebo on the side of the house. As we watched, a police photographer emerged from it holding an oversized camera and walked up to the open French windows of the house before disappearing inside.

Good, the body was still *in situ*. I turned around to Ross.

'Check where Tyson died,' I said, 'and stay out of sight.'

Ross moved off to investigate the shrubbery while I crept up the side of the garden.

'And for Hecate's sake don't eat anything you find,' I hissed at his back.

I was pretty sure Forensics would have cleaned up any poison, but I didn't want Ross's demise on my conscience.

It is important to visit the scene before it is released and current practice is that only those involved in the investigation can attend the scene. That's me, obvs, as well as Austey & Tenny. You are looking for anything foreign to the scene as well as fingerprints and other physical marks. The hard thing to spot is what's missing.

I entered the tent through the loosened flaps. It was not a pretty sight, though it's rarely the sight of death that bothers us professionals. Anyway, if you saw the mess I make of the birds and mice I catch you'd know that. What I discovered that day really makes me gag is the stink of dead human. And they don't smell great at the best of times.

Jo lay sprawled across the steps of the gazebo, her head resting across on the top level. Her face was a bloody mess, caused by a deep gash on the side of her left temple. But the bottle-blonde hair on the back of her head was also dark with blood. She was wearing a rather short green cotton summer dress and I could see fresh make-up and immaculately applied nail and toenail varnish. Her feet were bare and I guessed she'd taken her heels off to walk across the lawn. So far so pedestrian, no pun intended, I said to myself. But what was this thin horizontal fleshmark above the front of her right ankle?

I felt footsteps crossing the lawn towards me and retreated to the back of the tent looking for an escape gap, with Jo's lifeless staring eyes inches from my whiskers. I burrowed under the lower edge of the canvas and slipped out just as the front tent flap was flung open. I heard Austenson's gravelly voice.

'So you are saying she might have fallen, then?'

'It's certainly possible she slipped on the damp grass as she approached the gazebo,' said another voice. I took it to belong to the scene of crime forensic officer, SOCO in the trade.

'But is it likely?'

'Not unless she was running flat out, tripped and fell face down on the steps. Is that what you think happened?'

'Don't know yet. Does the temple wound match the step?'

'It does, but the evidence of blunt instrument trauma to the back of the head certainly doesn't.'

'Anything else?'

'Not at the moment. We need to get the body to the lab.'

'OK.'

I'd heard enough. I slipped quietly across the top of the gazebo as they walked back up to the house to start my own painstaking examination of the crime scene. After twenty minutes or so I'd almost given up the claw-tip search around the scene when I found something interesting. Six feet past the gazebo steps facing the tree side there was a line of half a dozen small but apparently deep holes in the grass, each around six inches from each other. Why were they there?

There was a miaow from the vegetation next to the fence on Carl Popper's side. I could see Ross's face peering out of some ferns up towards the house. I trotted across the grass into cover then up to him.

'What the bloody hell are you doing up here?'

'Well, you told me to keep out of sight. After I found the spot where Tyson was poisoned I thought I'd have a look around. Look what I found.'

He disappeared into the ferns and I followed him in. Behind, there was an area of flattened vegetation.

'This was Rosie's sleeping spot when it was hot,' he said.

I looked at him.

'Yes, she wasn't too bright. But this is new,' he said.

He was looking at an extra-large silver tent peg which had been hammered deep into the Kent chalk. From the top hung a few threads of nylon line.

'Wait here,' I said.

I rushed across the lawn to the fence opposite and dived into the border plants. Jo had favoured a seaside look and bamboo on this side, and there, behind the ornamental rushes, was another silver tent peg stuck deep in the ground.

Eureka. I had some idea of how, but the motive would need more work. But the murder weapon was clear to me.

🐈

Things were quiet over the next day and a half. I'd told Ross to question the pets of the main players. He'd spoken to Sappho, Rev. James's cat, and Cap, short for Capability, the Davis's Yorkie. Of course, nobody was mourning Tyson either but with him and Rosie now dead everybody wanted to help. It seemed that the Reverend spent an inordinate amount of time at the top of her church tower with a telescope, and not just at night. And Bill, an amateur photographer, had apparently developed a recent interest in insect macro shots.

Later that evening, after a last look at the crime scene again, I climbed the raised fence to look into the Davis' garden. Lisbet Davis was pruning the borders of the ultra-modern parterres, with their combination of perfect hedge symmetry, unusual plants from ex-colonial states in the compartments and sustainable rainbow-dyed path materials.

Ross, who had read up on this stuff, had taken me on a tour of her creation earlier that morning.

'She retains the obsession of modern gardens with geometry and architecture which runs through our culture from *les jardins à la francaise* to Roberto Marx,' he said, 'but not to the exclusion of plants themselves, and at the same time she incorporates the anger, anarchy and chaos of our time, as manifested by the decapitated statue of Churchill in the Farnese Hercules pose in the south-west corner and the great bronze frieze, displaying Greta Thunberg expelling Donald Trump from a heavenly Mar-a-Lago, diagonally opposite.'

'OK – I get it. She's unhinged,' I said, uncharitably.

'Well, possibly. But on the bright side, she plants *Nepeta Cataria*.'

'What?'

'Cat-nip,' he said, pointing his paw at the small dark-green plant in front of us. 'Tuck in.'

Now, as I watched the resident genius using a tape measure to measure out the distance between the hedges and plants to the millimetre, I noted that the garden contained other elements I hadn't noticed before, including disguised herb gardens on ornately distressed ladder planters and enormous solar-powered night torches. Lisbet looked up at the setting sun, spotted me and scowled before heading indoors. Something was scratching an itch in me.

'What are you up to, Flic?' said a now-familiar voice behind me.

I swivelled my head around. DI Austenson and Constable Tennyson were standing on the lawn, cigarettes in hand, looking up at me. Surprised, I slipped down the fence into the undergrowth and hid, peering out through the rushes.

'You've scared her off, guv,' said Tennyson.

'No matter. Let's start the mental reconstruction.'

'OK, guv. On the evening in question Mr Bill Davis was taking macro photographs of a bee fly on the fence adjoining

Ms Crawford's property. At 7.48pm the bee fly in question perched on the top of the fence for a moment and Mr Davis raised the camera on its monopole and took a remote cable picture into the adjoining garden. In so doing he captured Mr Carl Popper looking over his fence at number 11, in the direction of the victim's house.'

'And we don't think Davis was taking pictures of the victim sunbathing or in the hot tub?'

'There is no evidence of that on his hard drive. As a long-standing amateur photographer, he claims to have no interest in sex. To quote his statement, *'The only f-number I care about is on my Nikon D850'*. Plus his wife confirms it, guv.'

'OK, move on,' said Austenson.

'The wife also confirms that she called Mr Davis into the house a few minutes later for tea, after which he disappeared into his study and spent the whole evening in his study on Photoshop. Our photographer has checked his activity log and confirms this – and also gave Davis a few tips on layers, I understand.'

'Stick to the point, Alf. What about the wife?'

'Lisbet Davis claims to have spent the evening downstairs watching TV, popped upstairs to say goodnight to her husband about 10pm and went to bed. Says she heard nothing next door.'

'OK, and what does Carl Popper say?'

'He admits that he looked over the fence, but that he was only staring mournfully at the spot where his cat was slaughtered by Tyson. He claims Ms Crawford did not see him looking over. However, under intense questioning he did admit something of a hopeless unreciprocated infatuation with the victim. But it seems his heart was finally broken when she casually dropped his butchered cat round in a bin bag.'

'Did he kill her dog?'

'He claims he could never do that. And post-mortem suggests the dog was poisoned somewhat later, after 9pm.'

'Could just be the dog was a bit slow finding the poisoned meat. His movements?'

'The dog's?'

'Popper's, Constable. Keep up.'

'He claims he left the house at 8.15pm and met the other Whitstable Naturist Weight-loss Swimmers at 8.30 on Seasalter beach. They only swim on moonless nights to avoid body-shaming. His fellow overweight-but-not-obese swimmers confirm this, and that they all swam together until about 10.30pm, though socially distanced. He was home by 11.00pm.'

'So, we come to the ex-husband,' said Austenson.

'Yes, guv. Jonny Miro, owns a taxi firm. Ex-boxer, has form. Pickings a bit slow at present given the pandemic, so seemed at first a prime suspect. Came round to take the victim out to dinner. Says he just wanted to discuss re-negotiating the divorce settlement. But they got into an argument almost immediately and the victim got him to leave after barely ten minutes.'

'So he's also in the clear.'

'Yes, Guv, Rev. James has confirmed that she saw him through her telescope on top of the church both arrive and leave. She says he arrived at 8.35pm and left shortly thereafter. We know he was sitting outside The Ancient Poseidon pub at 9pm and did not leave till closing time.'

'The Rev. keeps a rather close eye on her flock, doesn't she? Why is she so certain of the precise time?'

'Her one-hour Christian Astronomy group meets in the church at 9pm and the members usually arrive a bit early so she checks her watch. After they left an hour later she went back up and spotted Ms Crawford's body on the steps. That's when she called us. We arrived 10 minutes later. That also means she has a watertight alibi.'

Tennyson closed his notebook. 'That's all, guv.'

'Well, it's clear then,' rasped Austenson.

'Guv?'

I miaowed from the rushes. I agreed with Jane and it was nearly time to present the other evidence. Darkness was falling rapidly over the gardens.

'Let's have a look at this cat,' said Austenson.

She stepped over the rushes to where I was lying, next to the silver tent peg.

'Hi there, sweetie... Hallo, what's this?'

Things happened quickly after that. Austenson bent down to examine the tent peg and I bit her index finger hard. She swore like a parade-ground sergeant and leapt back, shaking her hand as if it were on fire. While she did a passable dervish dance I raised myself slowly and ambled down the lawn, before stretching out on the grass. You have to be cruel to be kind sometimes.

After she'd run her hand under Jo's kitchen tap for ten minutes and found some plasters and Tennyson had made himself useful by finding the other tent peg, both of them walked down to where I lay and stared down at me licking my paws.

'I could kick her over those trees,' said Austenson.

'And I wouldn't breathe a word, guv, but you'd have to explain it to Ms Johns,' said Tennyson.

'I know,' said Austenson wistfully.

I held her gaze as I stood up to reveal the line of pole holes I'd been lying on. They were still examining them when the church clock sounded for 9.45pm. A few moments later the Davis garden was filled with yellow light. Austey and Tenny looked at one another and walked over to look over the fence.

When they came back I'd long gone. But I knew Austenson was smiling.

The following evening I was lying in Grace's lap while Jane Austenson brought her up to speed. They sat either side of the garden table at dusk, each sipping a glass of crisp white Chardonnay. Austenson was still wearing a plaster over her right index finger but at least it looked like she'd had a shower and changed her blouse.

'Lisbet Davis knew about Carl's Naturist Swimmers and Rev. James's Christian Astronomers because she's been a member of both groups,' she said, 'but more important she knew about Rev. James' peeping Thomasina predilections.'

'But how did she know that Jo would not go to dinner with Jonny?' said Grace.

'That was tricky until Jonny confessed he'd consulted Lisbet on what to say to Jo when he picked her up that evening. He followed her advice, came on all demanding about the settlement and was turfed out.'

'So with her husband upstairs playing with his Photoshop, the coast was clear for Lisbet. But how did she do it and why?'

'The how involved using two light but strong empty herb ladders to climb over the fence and down the other side. She carried over six extra-long solar fire-effect garden torches, two extra-duty strength tent pegs, a rubber tent mallet and a length of green low-visibility extra-strength nylon brick line especially ordered from the States, for use in construction and gardening. And her trusty tape-measure, of course.'

'Amazing – a criminal mastermind with uncanny military precision.'

'She had calculated the exact distance from the gazebo steps to place the nylon line and hammered in the tent pegs hidden in the borders with the rubber mallet so that the line was set at ankle height.'

I looked up at Grace's face, which was shining with admiration. I could have told you all this and more, I thought – if I could speak human. Jane continued playing Poirot.

'Of course, she poisoned Tyson first. Chucked over a prime fillet towards Popper's fence which was laced with ground-up metaldehyde.'

'Slug pellets?'

'You know your gardening, Grace.'

'Go on,' Grace said. She was blushing.

'Lisbet Davis then retreated to the other side of the gazebo and planted the six torches in the grass in a line three feet wide. At around 9.45pm, when the light level dropped, the torches flared on. From inside the house Jo would have thought the back of the gazebo was on fire.'

'So Jo rushes out, trips on the nylon line and dives head first into the concrete steps.'

'Yes, Lisbet thinks she's dead and rushes round to take up the tent pegs and line. She had about ten minutes before Rev. James returned to her telescope. But then it all went wrong.'

'How?' whispered Grace.

'Well, like many weekend campers, Lisbet had forgotten to take one of these.'

She reached in her pocket and pulled out an implement with a plastic handle and hook at the end of a thin length of steel.

'Is that a...' Grace said.

'Yes, it's a tent peg extractor – and you never have one when you need it. Without it the pegs were locked into the clay. Lisbet panicked, but she got the nylon string off and headed back past the gazebo, no doubt aiming to recover the pegs later. But then she must have heard Jo groan or show signs of life. She only had one option then. To pummel the back of Jo's head with the rubber mallet. Suffice to say, when we found the mallet buried under Lisbet's exquisite arabesque parterre there was no shortage of DNA.'

'Gory, but why kill Jo at all?'

'Because Jo had erected her high latticing so as not to be overlooked. That was bad, but the tipping point was her choosing fast-growing climbers which had just become visible from Lisbet's garden. When she confessed, Lisbet claimed Jo had destroyed her life's work.'

'What were the climbers?'

Jane pulled out her notebook.

'Yellow Clematis tangutica and Virginia creeper.'

'I see. Virginia creeper goes bright red in Autumn. It is a horrible combination, so it's understandable really,' said Grace.

'Understandable!' gasped Jane.

'I mean clematis and rambling rose would have been OK...'

Jane gave Grace a look and picked up her glass.

'You are an evil woman, Grace Johns,' she said, smiling.

I left them chuckling in the garden and climbed upstairs to watch the July sunset. I perched on the sill and thought about Ben, about seeing Grace happy again and about taste in plant colour co-ordination as a motive for murder. That was possibly a first in the annals of crime. But mostly I thought about the glorious colours in the sky as the glowing orb of the sun descended smoothly into the dark sea.

2

The Poossy Kentuka Corpse

Affair

IT DIDN'T TAKE LONG FOR THE NEXT CRIME SPREE TO HIT MY
cat basket. For several weeks since mid-April there had
been a spate of beehive thefts in the Canterbury area. Now,
more than a month later, Jane Austenson and her side kick
Alf Tennyson had almost gone spare carrying out night
stakeouts of hive sites in a futile attempt to apprehend the
bee-rustling gang. Each time they returned bleary-eyed from
some field deep in the Canterbury countryside they would
learn of another bee-napping in a different part of the district.

Back at HQ Austenson and Tennyson had rapidly gained
the nickname 'the bumbling ones' and were constantly being
asked about the success of their 'non-sting' operation. This
was doing nothing for Jane's mood when she visited the
house. She and Grace behaved like an item after the Gazebo
case, but necessary social distancing and the lack of progress
on the crimes were doing nothing to maintain their romance.
The team had no suspects, leads or intelligence from the

previous raids, so Jane was pulling her cropped hair out and as bad tempered as a lioness with a thorn in her claw.Then, as suddenly as it had begun, the plague of hive robberies ceased. By then, thirty-one had been purloined and the local small-scale honey producers had been decimated. Speculation about the case rumbled on in the local press for a day or two until it was blown away like an old cobweb with my discovery of a corpse yards from our back garden.

🐾

Since I needed somewhere quiet to cogitate, I had taken to scaling the fence behind the garden and dropping down into the dense undergrowth on our side of the Crab & Winkle path, which runs from Whitstable to Canterbury along the route of the old train line. For over a century until the 1950s whelks and oysters were transported on it from the harbour to the cathedral city's inns and pubs. Now there is blissful silence and you can find a tiny sun-dappled Arcadia in the midst of the tangled foliage around it with just the occasional chubby jogger panting by on the path below for unwelcome distraction. But on this occasion I had different company.

I had just found the perfect spot on a grass-covered mound between two shady trees when I noticed that there was someone else reposing a little below me, next to an overgrown thorn bush. At first I thought it might be the local vixen so I perked up sharpish in case she wanted an afternoon snack. But then I saw that this female mammal was wearing a blue waterproof jacket, jeans and walking boots, and looked altogether too relaxed for the location. She was stretched out on her back, her arms flung up either side of a mass of grey-blonde hair. The fingers of her hands were curled over as if beckoning me to her side.

I approached and sat beside her. Her face was not a pretty sight, swollen and peppered with a mass of red spots. I guessed her to be about fifty and, apart from her demise, apparently in good shape. She wore a wedding ring and had a gold-coloured watch on her left wrist so robbery gone wrong did not seem likely. Her sightless eyes were open and matched the fresh green leaves above her. Apart from her face, there were no obvious signs of assault.

I examined the gap in the foliage towards the Crab & Winkle path below. The grass and twigs in that direction had been displaced and pressed down. I guessed she had been very recently carried or dragged up the slope, perhaps in the middle of the night and dumped here. But she would be difficult to spot by a passer-by and might lie in this spot for days until some over-keen dog escaped his lead and sniffed his way up here. There was nothing for it. I'd have to go missing. I wearily made my way back to my resting spot and lay down to make myself comfortable. It was going to be a long wait.

Then I started my pitiful miaowing.

Grace and Jane finally found me and the body towards dusk. They were both wearing Jane's brash leather motorcycling gear to cope with the thorns and nettles in the wood, so when they burst through the foliage it looked like I was being rescued by a couple of multicoloured ninjas lost in the Amazon forest. Watch the bloody crime scene, you amateurs, I said to myself. After Grace had stopped squealing at the corpse I was quickly scooped up and whisked away by her while Jane secured the scene and called in the SOCOs. About bloody time, too. I was hoarse by then.

But more than ready to start my second murder investigation.

The following evening I was sitting in the armchair in the lounge while they sat on the sofa and talked about the victim. Nothing like a corpse to bring lovebirds together. Ross lay on his side on the rug, watching a TV documentary on the Chinese Cultural revolution. A typical intellectual, never in the moment. Yes, Mao killed a lot of people, but let's focus on the one behind the garden fence.

'The poor little thing must have been frightened to death, paralysed by that poor woman's body,' said Grace.

She was gazing at me tenderly.

'Hmm,' said Jane, eying me suspiciously.

'She's seen a lot of tragedy one way and another,' said Grace.

'Well, she certainly seems to be drawn to corpses,' said Jane.

Get to it, I thought to myself, avoiding Jane's stare while I cleaned my paws.

'The woman is Petra Cushing,' said Jane at last, 'she ran a tea and cake shop in town, which also sells branded upmarket food. It's called Cushing's Comforts.'

'I've seen it but never been in,' said Grace, 'it looks like it's for rich DFLs.'

Like many locals, Grace had an unhealthy contempt for Down-From-London types. She avoided any shop that looked as if it catered for them. It's true some either bought the monstrous new-build weekend pads springing up around the golf course and Tankerton slopes or just money-inundated the High Street and beach at weekends over the summer months. But she ignored the fact that the more normal types kept the High Street buzzing.

'Its prices aren't for the faint-hearted, that's true,' said Jane.

'What did she die of?'

'Anaphylactic shock, caused by numerous bee-stings. She was probably allergic to them.'

'That's awful,' said Grace.

'Thing is,' said Jane, 'it's obvious she was dumped by the Crab & Winkle when she could have been buried deep in the countryside, where she wouldn't be found for months. So someone was not too bothered if we found her.'

Good point, detective, but have you put two and two together yet, I mused.

'The other thing is, is there a connection between the murder and the hive robberies?' said Jane.

Eureka. There's hope for you yet, blondie.

'That sounds far-fetched. But where did she live?' asked Grace.

'A couple of hundred yards from here. She also owned the cake-maker by the railway line and lived above it.'

'Oh, you mean "Cake Station." Lovely sponges.'

I'd stopped licking and was hanging on every word. Jane looked over and I flicked my eyes over to the telly.

'You know, that cat...' said Jane.

'I know, she's uncanny, but she is just a moggy,' said Grace.

Butter would not melt in my mouth at that point. I mean, obviously – I'd spit it out. I'm lactose intolerant.

I sloped off the armchair and left them to it. Enough of this chit-chat – there was a murder to solve.

✦

Much later that evening I slipped out of the cat flap and headed out on my expedition to the Cake Station. It was a moonless night and I slipped through the gardens like a shadow until I reached the road running parallel to the railway line. Then I turned left and hugged the pavement's overgrown hedge until I reached a line of six houses almost opposite a narrow brick bridge. The last house was the Cake Station, a converted Victorian dairy shop. No way in at the front, but at the rear one of the ground floor sash windows had been left partly lifted, propped up by an old cake tin. I slipped into the house and found myself in the kitchen, which was replete with spotless stainless steel cupboards and surfaces. I guessed it got hot in there when Petra had baked her cakes. I stepped through the open doorway leading to the corridor and glanced both ways before bounding silently up the stairs. There, I found the door to the main bedroom ajar. Inside, I spotted Petra's desk next to the front-facing window and jumped up onto its surface. There were two open notebooks on it, one showing columns of financial calculations while the other was open at a page covered with the addresses of commercial premises. And in the corner of the desk was a jar of honey. I edged closer to read the label in the gloom. Kentuka.

'Can I help you?' said a deep voice behind me on the bed.

I jumped up and turned through 180 degrees in the same instant. A large black shape lying on the pale duvet was uncoiling itself with a liquid grace, his gold eyes filling with fire as he stood up. It was a cat, but unlike any I'd ever encountered. He was the largest Bengal I'd ever seen. Bengal, my arse – it was a bloody puma.

'Good evening, Ms,' he said, 'my name is Cerberus, and you are definitely in the wrong house.'

At the mention of the name I instinctively puffed myself up to the max and caterwauled as loudly as I could. Cerberus, aka the Tankerton Terror, the Widowmaker of Whelkville, a giant Bengal with a range so enormous that unspayed males in Herne Bay took themselves off to the vets so he wouldn't do the job on them without anesthesia. The windows shook and everyone within a range of a quarter of a mile was doubtless jolted out of their dreams. But I thought I was done for.

Cerberus looked at me quizzically until I finally finished. Slowly, he lifted an unsheathed claw to his mouth.

'Sshh,' he said evenly, 'please don't bother the neighbours. Accept your fate quietly.'

'Yes, pipe down, Flic,' said a squeaky voice from the doorway.

Cerberus and I glanced across at the source. Ross was peering around the door.

'Christ, Ross, is she with you?' said Cerberus.

''Fraid so,' said Ross, 'she's investigating the killing of your human.'

I felt the words shake the colossus in front of me. He dropped flat onto the bed as if he'd been shot.

'Petra… killed?' he whispered.

And the golden fire in his eyes was extinguished in that moment.

Much later, Ross and I walked home in the early morning light. My irritation and relief mixed themselves up until I could contain myself no longer.

'Why the bloody hell didn't you tell me you were following me?'

'If I'm going to be your oppo then I need to practise the skills, including tailing,' Ross said.

'So you *were* listening to Jane earlier?'

'Of course. Being invisible in plain sight and following unseen is all part of it. Not something a part-ginger cat like you can do – that would be like being followed by a traffic bollard.'

'Hmmm, I'm tricolour calico so less of the cheek. Still, Cerberus turned out to be helpful. So Petra was storing masses of this Kentuka honey which has only recently appeared in the shops frequented by the DFLs, selling at a hundred quid a jar. She was also planning a dramatic expansion of Cake Station pop-ups. I'm sure there is a connection to the beehive heists. But what is it?'

'Could Petra have been killed for not revealing the source of the Kentuka honey?' said Ross.

Why use bee-stings in that case? But I didn't make the point to him. The adrenalin had suddenly worn off and a great weariness swept over me. I wanted to thank Ross for saving me by rubbing my head against his. But of course I didn't. It would have been completely unprofessional while the killer was out there.

The following morning was a total washout, with torrential

rain streaming down the windows and intermittent thunder and lightning. Once both Jane and Grace had left for work, we immersed ourselves in research, Ross in the study on the desktop and me on Jane's iPad in the lounge. We'd arranged to meet Cerberus for lunch and at 1pm the food dispenser popped open and we stopped to compare notes. We both froze to the sound of plastic being wrenched apart in the utility room followed by the scratching of litter from our tray. The potent stench hit us just before Cerberus entered the kitchen and stretched himself out on the floor.

'I wouldn't go in there for a bit,' he said nodding towards the utility room, 'and your cat flap needs looking at.'

We stared at him and then down at the open dispensers.

'Carry on. I've eaten – fresh,' he said with contempt.

I looked at Ross. He rolled his eyes.

'What did you learn?' I asked.

'First, there is only one type of honey bee in the UK, so it follows that all honey bees can produce Kentuka honey,' said Ross.

'So, it may be that the Kentuka company was trying to boost production of its honey by placing stolen hives close to Kentuka bushes,' I said.

'The physical source of the Kentuka company's honey is a closely guarded trade secret. But the murder might suggest that the Kentuka bushes are nearby and their location was known to Petra Cushing. She might also have known about the stolen hives.'

'What do we know about the Kentuka plant?'

Ross puffed himself up to lecture me. I do hate that.

'*Leptospermum pretiosabovisstercus* was developed from a shrub which originated in Australia and was brought to England in the mid-1800s by Victorian naturalist Lord Lee of Bruce. Forest fires have wiped that shrub out in Australia. It's supposed to have extraordinary healing properties. It's claimed it can cure all First World ills, from restoring hair to making corns disappear and everything in-between.'

'What did Aboriginal people use it for?'

'What you'd expect. Fungal toe and dingo bites. And as food of course. Anyway, it was thought extinct as it could not survive English winter frosts.'

'But it wasn't.'

'No. The original shrub had been saved in a hidden greenhouse in a Cornish micro-climate on the Bruce estate. Cuttings were taken and the plant was preserved, though forgotten. A few years ago, Lord Lee's descendant, the eccentric cultivar Christophe Lee, announced that he had developed a new distinctive, purple-flowered variety of the Kentuka plant which would be used for the production of honey with anti-bacterial qualities.'

'I dimly remember. Wasn't there a crazy bidding war for the right to license the plant?'

'Yes. That's when Christophe Lee went to ground with all his Kentuka shrubs. The only sign he exists is the small supply of Kentuka honey to the Canterbury area.'

'Why did he disappear?'

'It seems that his fear was that after licensing his plants the honey would be adulterated with only a small Kentuka plant content and unsubstantiated claims would be made about its properties.'

'He had a point. So, both he and the Kentuka plants are out there somewhere,' I said.

'Well, that's all I've got. What did you discover?' said Ross.

'I checked Petra Cushing out,' I said.

'Find anything?'

'Who she was married to, despite living alone. She wore a wedding ring, remember. So the husband is a possible suspect.'

Cerberus growled from his reclining position.

'No one mentioned a husband. Perhaps she was a widow,' said Ross.

'She was married to a guy called Christophe Lee.'

Ross choked on his mouthful of cat biscuits.

'Christophe Lee was her husband?' he gasped.

'Yep. And I think they just lived apart. There was no divorce.'

We looked across at Cerberus.

'I haven't met him. They have lived apart since well before my time, though they spoke often on the phone,' he said.

'Anything else?' I asked.

'She visited him every other Thursday. Took him shopping and clean washing sometimes. She walked so it wasn't that far,' he answered.

'So he probably lives locally,' said Ross.

'I think so, but how do we locate him?' I said.

'I can do it.' said Cerberus.

Ross and I nodded – cats don't recognise faces. Only he would remember the voice on the phone and the smell of the clothes Petra washed. He might also pick up traces of Petra Cushing's scent.

'And when I do...' said Cerberus. He bared his fangs.

'When you do, you'll report back. He might well be innocent.'

I'd surprised myself with my sudden hard tone. But

Cerberus smiled and stood up.

'Sure, girl,' he said, leaving the room.

We heard him squeeze himself through the broken cat flap. I made a mental note to make myself scarce when Grace found both it and his handiwork in the tray.

It didn't take Cerberus long to find Christophe Lee's hideout. A day later he was back, elbowing aside the temporary obstruction Grace had constructed around the cat-flap to keep out 'a bloody fox or badger or something.' After taking another seizure-inducing dump in the fresh litter and drinking all our water he flopped into Grace's armchair. I noticed his face looked wrong.

'I've found it,' he said at last.

'Where?'

'Abbott's Farm, just north of Chestfield. It and the adjoining field are surrounded by a high hedge and inside that there are a bunch of greenhouses. I got chased out of one of them by a whole bloody bee swarm.'

'Did you see Lee?'

'Yes, before that, through a window sitting at his kitchen table. Couple of blokes with him. They seemed to be guarding him.'

He was nodding off and I inched forward to look at him close-up. His front paws and nose were badly swollen. He wasn't invulnerable after all.

'OK, rest now, let the bee-sting poison wear off,' I said.

'They were only tiny sods,' he slurred, 'but too many of them. They chased me halfway back.'

He was all in. He spoke almost to himself.

'Funny thing, the plants in the greenhouses were all in water.'

And he was out like a light.

At midnight, the three of us were sitting on a tree branch looking into Christophe Lee's kitchen window. Two men sitting with him were playing X-Box on the table, their eyes on a battered corner TV. Christophe himself was tied to a high-backed chair and sitting in front of a bunch of torn-up papers. This was not a Covid-rules compliant household and it looked like we were just in time.

'Stay here – I'm going a bit closer to listen,' I said.

'No way,' said Cerberus and Ross in unison.

'We can't all perch outside that window,' I replied.

A minute later I'd climbed up to the sill and was leaning against the side brickwork, hoping my gingery pelt would blend in with it.

Stakeouts are usually tedious and pointless affairs, resulting in no new information and a stiff neck, but I was lucky. Ten minutes later, a large white Range Rover came up the farm track and two people got out. Moments later, a burly man and a raven-haired woman entered the kitchen. The man was just another rent-a-thug but the woman's face shocked me. It had graced the first page of a hundred forgettable websites. It was Selma Dudds.

But the cleansed and humidified features that had once dominated the global influencer market were now screwed into a scowl distorted by a thousand untested face creams.

As the owner of the 'inner fullness' brand POOSSY she had transformed the lives of thousands of really wealthy women. Her lifestyle slogans like 'inspirational, aspirational and genitalianal' and 'good intentions definitely smell like my privates' had given an exfoliating bleach enema to the English language and scientific fact but you had to respect her success. Not.

Now she loomed over Christophe Lee like the vampiric character she had played in her 'Red Caviar Juice' online ad while he blanched and recoiled. Quite right – she wasn't socially distancing properly, but that was the least of his problems.

'Why haven't you signed the licence agreement?' she said sweetly.

'I can't,' he said.

'No, of course not,' she said.

She nodded at the heavies, who untied the captive. He massaged his wrists.

'No,' he said, 'I mean, I can't let you make unscientific claims about Kentuka honey. I won't sign it.'

Dudds shrugged. She lifted her pink scrotal sac-shaped handbag onto the table and dispersed its contents on the surface.

'All right. I guess we'll just have to go through the proposed product range again.'

'Please God, no,' gasped Christophe Lee.

'Or we can try the face mask, like we did with Petra. Kentuka, yoghurt, oats, berries, alpine flowers.'

Christ, that's an expensive breakfast, I thought.

'You killed Petra with that bloody face mask. She was allergic to bee stings,' Christophe shouted.

43

'It was a karma accident. You shouldn't have had the windows open. It's you who keeps killer bees illegally, not me. And if you'd signed the licence agreement I'd never have had to force her to experience the facial range.'

I didn't hear the rest against Lee's loud sobbing. Dudds waited until he'd quietened, then she picked up a thick rose-coloured candle.

'So this is what we call our new *c-anal-dle* product. You douse it with Kentuka honey and paprika and light it until the scent permeates the room. Then you blow it out and apply it. It is a proven product for lady haemorrhoids but I'm sure it also works for men...'

I couldn't hear much more after that because of his screams, but somehow he held out and didn't sign. After a while even I couldn't take it any more. I slipped down the wall to where Ross and Cerberus were waiting. I told them what I'd witnessed while they winced.

'It's the bravest thing I've ever seen,' I said, 'we have to save him even if he's done wrong.'

'Yes, but how?' said Cerberus.

'I have a plan,' I said, 'and I think you are going to like it.'

The following day was Sunday. At about 2pm, three of the Faversham Freewheelers cycling club, Kurt Chain, Amy Wingnut and Brian Cones were standing at the edge of Rumour's Wood Down fixing a puncture on Kurt's bike. Their inane bragging about their respective Strava scores was rudely interrupted by a deep unholy growling coming from the pines. They turned to see a large dark shape moving through the fern cover towards them. By the time it reached the road the three lycra wearers were demonstrating their sprinting skills without their bikes, screaming as they fled down the hill towards Boulder's Bottom. When they finally turned to look back up the road, they saw something Brian later described on the Whitstable's Community Forum's Facebook page as 'the bloody panther in Junglebook.' Amy's blurry maximum magnification phone picture of the feline monster playfully turning the front wheel of Kurt's upturned bike had the highest liked score on the page.

The following morning the local postman Jimi Pannier heard growling in the hedge next to No 3 Railway Cottages in the hamlet of Gibson's Neck and bent over to look. The horror picture on *Kentish Digest* online a few hours later, displaying Pannier's neatly raked face, with deep diagonal scratches, convinced all sceptical locals they had a big cat on their hands. That and Pannier's union rep demanding police protection for any deliveries north of Chestfield. Later that afternoon, local detectorist Janis Shifter reported seeing a large puma-like animal carrying off her ham baguette lunch while she attended a call of nature. During her TV interview she thanked God that the puma had not damaged 'her very sensitive equipment.'

The clip went viral and by then the story was national. Local wild animal parks were forced to deny any of their big cats had escaped, and BBC naturalist Robert Gusset speculated on the possible release of a puma as being the last 'charitable' act of a private collector dying of Covid-19.

The authorities knew something had to be done to stop the panic. The local police superintendent got the call that evening.

The following morning over a hundred coppers started beating the fields between the three points where the big cat had been sighted. Just before midday they reached Abbott's Farm and Jane Austenson knocked on the door.

🐈

Jane was lying on the sofa in the lounge, her face covered in crotamiton cream. Not Kentuka honey, thank Bastet.

'We were lucky,' she said.

'Not exactly,' said Grace. She had applied the cream with complete disregard to the Government's guidelines. This was definitely love.

'When they saw us, Dudds's heavies panicked and made a run for their car. While we stopped them she sneaked into one of the greenhouses. Or rather they were hydroponic tanks disguised as battered old greenhouses. Packed with flowering Kentuka plants.'

'So that's where she was caught?'

Jane sighed.

'When we arrived Dudds had just been applying Kentuka honey to herself to demonstrate some weird naturist depilation technique to Christophe Lee. Incidentally, I don't think he'll ever recover from her torture – the poor guy seems broken.'

'I suppose the bees went crazy when she went in the greenhouse,' said Jane.

'And then some. She was covered from head to foot when we reached her.'

'You were very brave to drag her out.'

'I was braver having to listen to her woke hippy narcissistic crap before she was finally sedated,' said Grace.

'Did she say anything else?

'Oh, something about apitherapy not being all it's cracked up to be. She was rambling a bit from the stings.'

'What was her plan?'

'She eventually admitted telling her heavies where to dump Petra's body after the accident. I'm sure she wanted her to be found. Once they'd got Christophe to sign a backdated sole licence agreement they would probably have faked his remorseful suicide for accidentally killing her. Then she'd own the Kentuka plant rights. But we'll never prove it. She's still looking at a year or two without fennel-scented sex toys and batshit facials but I'm sure she'll be back.'

'What about Christophe?'

'He admitted to importing Puerto Rican killer bees illegally. He was sure that they were less aggressive than Brazilian or Mexican ones. How wrong can a guy be?'

'But why?'

'It's the honey industry's dirty secret – they love killer bees. They are small but produce twice as much honey compared to European bees and they are resistant to mites. Christophe needed more Kentuka honey to sell to fund his hydroponic research and Petra wanted to take Cake Station global. She kept away from Abbott's Farm as much as possible as she was allergic to bee stings.'

'And the stolen hives?'

'Killer bee drones also mate with the queens of European beehives. They pass on their genes, which wipes out domestic colonies. To hide that Christophe had to steal the local hives and place them in his hydroponic tank greenhouses.'

'What will happen to the bees?'

'We rounded them up – as many as we could. They are

already on their way back to Puerto Rico. Unfortunately, we are forcing emigration on the kidnapped ones – poor sods.'

'I suppose Christophe gets off pretty lightly?'

'He wants out, so he made a deal with Wantsum Planet, the big hydroponics operation. I think that was his plan all along. They fund his legal defence and pay off the bee-keepers who lost their hives. In return he licenses his Kentuka plant to them exclusively. I bet in a few years they'll win the Queen's Award for Industry and he'll be given a CBE. All this mess will be quietly forgotten.'

'And the puma?'

'No trace anywhere, probably starved in the woods. Useful though, wasn't it?'

She glanced across at me.

I looked out of the window. You ain't getting anything from me, sister.

I got up and wandered outside. Ross was sitting on the fence looking into the neighbours' garden. He looked down at me.

'So it's worked,' he said.

'Cerberus?'

'Yes, he's been adopted by the couple at No. 2, Erica and Ernie. Only, get this, they call him Lucifurr.'

I smiled – as much as a feline can, anyway. It would be good to have Lucifurr around for future cases. Just then I noticed a bee performing a neat little salsa mid-air and alighting on the purple Cosmos flower next to me. It was small, much too small, but it had all the moves.

Respect, brother, I whispered. I edged away and thought again about the case while in the distance the traffic whistled sadly by on the Thanet Way. The crime was just the regular filthy tale of unhappy endings in this seaside Babylon. But the big picture was of a country of garden greenhouse scientists who have to change the world no matter what it costs them. And a layer cake of overlapping waves of immigrants continuously bringing us something new we didn't know we needed yet. In this case, Kentuka honey for the masses and fragrant candles for rich arses.

Sounds about right.

3

The Strange Case Of The Very

Useful Gastropods

I BARELY HAD TIME TO RECOVER FROM THE KENTUKA AFFAIR before the death of Jack McWally hit the nationals and gained blanket TV coverage. Jack had broken into the national football squad shortly before his death. He could actually see more than two passes ahead on the pitch, which was pretty unique as British footballers go. He had lived in one of the residential monstrosities springing up around the local golf course. However, if he ever tried to play a round, he'd be surrounded in seconds by half of Whitstable. There hadn't been a local hero this big since Hengist in the fifties. The four hundred and fifties. And Channel-hopping immigrants weren't quite so popular these days.

So there was nothing for it but to lie around until DI Jane Austenson, Grace's no-longer-distanced detective lover, told us all the gory details of the case. I didn't have to wait long. And lying around is what cats do best.

Jane finally came around for a coffee the following evening, looking her usual grim-faced and dishevelled self. Someone on the force had revealed details of Jack's death to the nationals and they'd splashed them out without restraint. He had been found hung by his signature branded laces from one of the exposed beams in his luxury home, wearing his old Whelkies football kit. The press had concluded that it was yet another sad case of inability to take sudden celebrity and the screaming commentariat had bought the suicide story. Jane and her constable, Alf Tennyson, were under enormous pressure to fall in with the prevailing narrative.

'Something is not right though,' said Jane, 'I can feel it in my gut.'

She proceeded to fill that gut with Grace's Famous Grouse.

I understood the stress she was under, what with Jack's ex-partners and acquaintances falling out of the woodwork with their 'well, he did seem very depressed at the invasion of his private life' press stories, picking up their fifteen minutes of infamy and several thousand more followers on the way to stereotyping another working-class lad.

There was no way I could visit the crime scene but fortunately I didn't need to. Thanks to the change in Government policy Jane and Grace had formed a two-adult bubble with Jane now often staying overnight. Earlier that evening I'd noticed her re-reading her notes in the downstairs study before going to bed. So Ross and I crept into the room later and sat on the desk top, slowly flicking over the pages of the file. We are great night readers of course. We are near-sighted, see in the dark, don't blink and are wide-awake at night – try that for size, *homo sapiens*.

The corpse pictures of the scene were not as expected. Jack's neck had not broken and the strangulation marks did not seem deep enough to cause oxygen depletion to the brain. And we cats are the real experts in throat strangulation. Forensics also stated he had recently eaten a dinner of gastropods, presently unidentified, and that the kitchen showed evidence of recent cooking activity. I was already sure that poisoning was the real cause of death.

The notes also revealed that Jack had not only bought the £2m house overlooking the beach but had also purchased a small section of the foreshore between Whitstable and Seasalter beaches, the prior ownership of which appeared to have been forgotten in the annals of time. This section of beach was some distance westward from his house. In addition, he had quietly received planning permission to lay a series of large, indented rocks on it between the high and low-water tidal marks, to supplement those already there. Curiouser and curiouser.

'Look at this,' said Ross.

The white sock of his left paw slid across a legal document that Jane had set aside on the desk. It documented the creation six months earlier of WTSC Ltd, a company in the 'health products business'. I scanned the names of the company directors. They were Jack, Donna McWally, his sister, and her husband Dr Zane Dicey. Jane's notes revealed that Dicey was an aerodynamics lecturer and consultant.

'Well, we know who to investigate next,' I said.

'And they live next to the cemetery, easy peasy,' said Ross.

By about 3am we'd digested the file and spread out all the photos again. Jack's picture when he'd played for the

Whelkies as an eleven-year-old, then a little later when he'd been picked after a scramble for his signature between the Big Six. In both he appeared a shy boy, unsmiling and nervous. The most recent portraits presented quite a contrast, showing him radiantly happy receiving a local honour at his old secondary school only the previous month. His dazzling smile dominated the picture. That old uncertain feeling was nagging at me again.

'Difficult to believe he'd end up as he did,' said Ross.

I didn't reply. I looked again at a scene of death picture of Jack's legs. No, there was no way he had killed himself.

'OK,' I said, looking at Ross. 'Best clear up,' I said, 'we have a full day tomorrow and we need our fourteen hours.'

The following afternoon found me sitting on the fence at the end of the McWally-Dicey residence. The garden backed onto the cemetery, so no human would be surprised to see a stray cat about. Back at our place, Ross had been deputised to do some research on our suspects, especially Dr Dicey. I was watching Dicey and Jack's sister sitting in their garden and about to make my own judgement.

Donna was slumped forward, her head in her hands, with Zane stroking her shoulder sympathetically, when the front doorbell rang. Zane got up to answer and a few moments later walked back into the garden with the considerable bulk and rotund features of Whitstable's celebrity cook, Mick Pollock, behind him. You could have knocked me off my perch with his smallest *amuse bouche*.

Pollock has a colourful back story, including a criminal

record as an over-enthusiastic debt-collector for local villains. Eventually convicted, he had taken up cooking whilst in prison, where he could also harm dead things.

His revolutionary introduction of extra-virgin engine oil and gold mig-welded ingredients into the menu of his London restaurant 'The Oily Rag' had catapulted him into the premier league of the planet's haute cuisine. Two years previously he had taken over the ailing Whitstable Whelk Co. and transformed its restaurant, renamed 'The Swearbox', into the El Bulli of the south coast. The restaurant critics were now salivating with expectation at his next invention, after the triumph of his signature dish, petrol-flambeed whelks in wiper fluid consommé.

So what was he doing here? Surely he had bigger whelks to fry? He certainly didn't hang about spending time on condolences for the grieving Donna.

'When the f*** do I get my hands on that f******* beach?' he barked at her.

'Come on, Mick, have a thought for what Donna's going through,' said Dicey, 'ease off on the language.'

'I don't give a bleeding monkey's,' said Pollock, 'her f****** brother promised to sell me the beach once he had no use for it.'

This was clearly too much for Donna.

'For God's sake, stop swearing and shouting. Jack's body is still warm and we don't even know what his will says. And he'd never sell to you and neither will I!' she cried.

'Don't take me for a f****** fool – of course he'll leave it to you. Who else did he have, the sad git. And you'll pass it onto me, or else knowledge of Zane's little private activities will be in the next anonymous email to the press.'

He turned and leaned close to Zane's face. The smaller man leaned back, no doubt to avoid Pollock's appalling whelky breath. I could smell it from the fence.

'And don't tell me not to swear, brainbox – do you think my customers would book six months in advance to come to The Swearbox unless they got insulted and humiliated by me at their tables? Bugger the food, that's my USP, you four-eyed toss**. It's never about the taste – it's always about the experience.'

He drew back and smoothed down his chef's jacket, which was seemingly covered in axle grease and oil stains. But the effing and blinding seemed to have calmed him down and he suddenly smiled benignly at the shattered couple.

'Well, anyway, enough of the head chef's tutorial. I'm sure you get the message. Let me know when you are in a position to sign the transfer of ownership. If not, remember I also have a very large, very hot whelk vat back at the restaurant. Somewhere to throw yourselves in once I expose you.'

After he had left I watched Zane consoling Donna in the garden. My mind was working overtime. It didn't sound as if Pollock had killed Jack and I had other reasons for doubting it anyway. Zane and Donna, on the other hand, appeared genuinely distraught. But if not them, who else had had motive and opportunity?

It was time to head back to the drawing board and see whether Ross had dug anything up. But I also mused we might need to bring Lucifurr, next door's Bengal cat, into play on this one.

When I returned, Ross was slumbering in my afternoon bed under the armchair in the study. I looked at him for a moment, the dark M of his forehead markings prominent against the handsome grey stripes of his thick coat. I thought what a shame it was he didn't have a bit more oomph. Then I caught myself and slapped him hard round the chops. He jumped up and was halfway out of the room before he slammed on the brakes and looked around.

'What the hell...' he said.

'I don't want your mangy pelt in my bed,' I replied.

'I've been on that bloody desktop all morning, Flic. I needed a rest.'

'It's not good to fall asleep on the job,' I replied. 'What did you dig up, if anything?'

He shook his head in disbelief and leapt onto the desk with as much dignity as he could muster. I settled down in my armchair to watch the show as the computer screen re-emerged from sleep mode. I was looking at a picture of Dr Zane Dicey.

'As we know, Dr Dicey is a scientist in the field of aerodynamics, so I looked at his most recently published papers. They are all about composites for jet plane structures and specialist uses like Formula 1 cars.'

'You mean like graphene?' I asked.

'That's right, carbon fibres of various types.'

'I can't see the connection to Jack's death, the beach purchase or the rocks he put on it. Have you got anything else?'

'Two things. Dr Zane left his university job this year and has stopped consulting for both the aviation industry and Formula 1. He's currently unemployed and so is his wife, Donna.'

'Hmm. What's the other thing?'

This was getting more interesting. Ross pressed down the mouse button and a photograph flashed up of a demonstration being broken up opposite No. 10. In it, Donna was being hauled off by a helmet-less copper.

'This photo is a year old. Both Donna and Zane are active in the whelk protection movement. In fact, they are fanatical in their opposition to intensive whelk fishing. Donna got charged with affray after this. Jack bailed her out and paid for a brief when she went to court. She got off with a suspended sentence.'

'Nothing wrong with what she's doing,' I said.

'Sure, some of my best friends are fanatical about animals.'

I couldn't help wondering what it was that Pollock had on Zane Dicey that would so embarrass him. What was this 'private activity' he'd mentioned?

It was a lot to think about. We had a couple of probably innocent and broke whelk-lovers, one of whom had abandoned his chosen field, and a dodgy celebrity chef who wanted a beach that the victim had owned. You'd think Donna and Zane would want to sell it in a flash. Instead, they were holding back. It wasn't like Pollock was a polluter. Apart from the engine oil, axle grease and brake fluids in the food, of course.

Still, the next step was obvious.

'Get Lucifurr round here. We've got a job for the boy.'

Ross clicked the mouse and the screen greyed over.

'And good work by the way,' I said.

Ross beamed with pride. Well, it doesn't hurt to throw him a morsel every so often, does it?

The three of us had been rooting in Grace's bedroom cupboards and drawers for about half an hour looking for it. Well, two of us had. Lucifurr, the oversized Bengal from next door, had been licking himself clean on her bed with all the insouciance of a sultan, his short black fur as disgustingly healthy as it could possibly be. Or as my mum used to say, shiny black don't slack. The local bird population, however, was undergoing a steep decline to keep him looking this good. He caught me staring at him and winked.

'Like what you see, girl?' he said.

Ginger brethren can't redden. Something my human Ben used to say to build up my confidence.

'We'd like a hand from you finding this thing,' I replied.

'Hell, you know where she keeps her stuff, girl.'

'I've found it!' said Ross from within the fitted wall cupboard.

Lucifurr and I followed him into the near-darkness. There, at the back with Grace's wetsuit and snorkelling gear, lay her diving accessories, including the small action camera she'd bought for her underwater filming. Even better, it was still attached to the floating handle. Like so many humans Grace was untidy and lazy. Her idea of clearing up was to chuck everything in a cupboard. Thank Menhit she didn't have to conceal her faeces.

Ross flicked the tiny camera out onto the carpet and I managed to switch it on. Only two bars of battery life remained. But the touchscreen was easy to navigate and Lucifurr soon got the drift of it. After ten minutes he switched it off and clamped his ivories around the soft handle, lifting it off the ground.

'OK, I've got it,' he gurgled.

'Remember,' I said, 'don't switch it on till you get there or there won't be any battery left. According to the online reviews its low light image is rubbish so wait until after dawn to start filming.'

Lucifurr nodded and strode magisterially out of the room. Ross and I looked around the bedroom and at each other. The place looked as if it had been ransacked by Vikings.

I sighed.

'It's good practice to conceal a covert search,' I said hopefully.

'Get lost – I've done my bit,' he replied.

And with that he was out of the door as well.

That evening, I reviewed the case whilst sitting on the back of the sofa in the spare bedroom, looking out over the houses untidily arrayed on the descending hillside. The red and orange hues of the Whelkville sunset sky loomed over the town like some celestial fire. It was a strange one, this case. Perhaps there was more to the some of the players than met the eye.

Then I heard some commotion downstairs and descended to find out what was up. Grace was sitting with Jane watching the local news. Ross lay on his back on the rug, watching the broadcast upside down with his legs spread out. Show some decorum, for Freyja's cat-driven chariot's sake.

On the screen, there was blurry mobile-phone footage of Mick Pollock being marched out of The Swearbox with a blanket over his head, his identity nevertheless revealed by his filthy chef's smock. That and the fact he was cussing like a good one, the sound coverage being repeatedly bleeped as he was bundled into the police car.

The footage cut to a police press conference chaired by a senior police suit, while an uncomfortable-looking Jane sat beside him answering questions. She confirmed that Jack McWally had in fact been killed by poison in his sautéed whelks and that his branded elasticated bootlaces could not have done the job of suffocating him.

I glanced across at Jane, who looked like she wanted to hide under the rug. The TV picture cut to a view of Whitstable's pebbled beach and the reporter's voiceover.

'Sources report that Jack McWally was in commercial negotiations with the celebrity chef to sell him part of Whitstable's beachfront the footballer had purchased late last year. It is well-known that Mr Pollock's ambition is to own all the gastropodic potential of the area. Indeed, some of his local detractors are already pointing out he wanted the town to become known as 'Whelkstable'. The forthcoming court case will show whether his well-known crabby temper and his desire to spread his tentacles even further into the community led to a fishy outcome in this sad case. And back to you in the studio, Abby.'

The screen turned black. We all turned to look at Jane holding the remote. She was staring at Grace.

'I told them it doesn't add up. Why would Pollock kill Jack when he was still in negotiations with him? Or make himself such an obvious suspect?' she said.

'Then why has he been arrested?' said Grace.

'Because it was taken out of my hands, that's why. Because

he visited Jack on the night of the murder and Jack was killed by bloody poisoned sautéed whelks,' Jane shouted.

She dropped the remote onto the sofa and got up.

'Sorry, I'm all in. Listen, I'm out of here. I'll see you tomorrow.'

After she had left, Grace made herself a very large whiskey and stared unseeingly at the moving pictures on the screen for a long time, with Ross purring in her lap. I went back upstairs to my viewing point and gazed down at the twinkling lights of the houses and the darkness of the water beyond.

Lucifurr rolled into the house around lunchtime the following day. He smelt of brine and dry seaweed and his coat now had a matted sun-dried look. He deposited the action cam on the kitchen floor and sauntered over to drink from our water bowl.

'I'm glad that's over,' he said.

'What happened?' said Ross.

'I nearly bleeding drowned, that's what happened,' he miaowed.

'Slow down, who was about when you got down there?' I said.

'I got to the beach just after dawn. The tide was starting to edge in over the rocks and there was a woman scraping away on one of them, surrounded by heavy duty plastic sacks. She had a couple of staffies loose, sniffing around on the beach. I thought she was some beach forager getting herself some winkles for breakfast and taking the dogs out at the same time. Then I realised she was replacing what she was picking with something else.'

'That doesn't make any sense,' said Ross.

'Anyway, I switched the action cam on and crept around the dogs to have a better look. Eventually I was well past her, filming from the rocks close to the water. She was definitely substituting one set of shelled slugs or whatever for another.'

'Then what happened?' I said.

'Well, it got light really quick and one of the staffies looked up and saw me. They both started barking and I realised I was cut off from shore. The woman looked around and saw me with the action cam in my mouth. She stood up and started walking over doing all that "here kitty" shit. There was only one thing for it – I dived off the last rock and swam out to sea.'

'As only Bengals can,' said Ross.

'Did the dogs follow you out?' I said.

'Staffies can't swim,' said Ross, 'heads are too heavy. All that crunching hardware, you see.

'The woman shouted at me for a bit with the dogs barking away behind her dementedly. I paddled around offshore hoping the current would carry me off somewhere safe before I shipped too much seawater down my gullet. But she suddenly gave up, gathered up her sacks and hurried off the beach. I swam ashore as soon as I was sure she really had gone.'

'Well done you. We'd better look at that film,' I said.

We transferred the video to the iPad with the WiFi connector and settled down to watch. The early shots were dark and grainy, but the footage of the young woman kneeling on the rocks was clear enough. Zooming in, we could see that she was scraping off limpets and throwing them in a bag. She was replacing them with shelled slugs, but what were they?

The final part of the film showed only jerky footage of rock and seaweed as Lucifurr turned and ran towards the water. Then there was a pause as he stopped at the edge and the film suddenly ended.

'I turned off the cam before I jumped in. To save the battery,' he said.

Ross piped up.

'Good thinking. Wind back to the last few seconds, Flic' he said.

I did as he asked.

'Freeze there,' he said.

'OK.'

We were staring at a clump of sea-weedy rock with some slugs on it.

'Zoom in,' said Ross.

'Surely that's not a whelk,' I said, spreading my paws across the screen.

'Yes, it is,' he answered, 'but not the common whelk, *Buccinum undatum.* The water is far too shallow for them. It's lighter coloured and smaller. It is *Nucella lapillus,* aka the dog whelk.'

'Why is she replacing limpets with dog whelks?' said Lucifurr.

'Is this Pollock's new gastronomic delight?' I asked.

'God no,' said Ross. 'You can't eat the little sods. It's what you can make with them.'

Lucifurr and I looked at one another with incomprehension. Ross sat back with a contented look.

'OK. Let's have the dog whelk 101 lecture,' he said.

Christ, not again, I said to myself, settling down for another marathon bore.

After Ross had explained the significance of dog whelks, we spent the next few hours doing electronic gumshoe work. Whelkville is full of artists of all sorts so it took a while, but in the end we found a suspect who fit the bill. Regan Ermine, the infamous painter of obscene illuminated manuscripts and textiles. Better still, we had recent pap shots of her coming out of The Swearbox with Jack.

The next step was to bring her out into the open. I put my plan, 'Operation Winkle Out', into action. Ross edited the video evidence and sent it via an untraceable web location to Kent Police HQ. Over the next few days, Lucifurr collected and deposited a limpet shell on Ermine's doorstep late every night. Then, having put the wind up her, we staked out Donna and Zane's place and waited for Ermine to crack.

Meanwhile, the police operation seemed to be going from bad to worse. As Jane had anticipated, the circumstantial evidence was not enough to charge Pollock. After four days of questioning, the interrogating officers were on PTSD-related home leave recovering from his incessant verbal abuse. Jane was fully back in charge of the case, but she had to get a quick result.

Late on the Sunday evening, five days after Jack's murder, Ermine stepped out of her car and knocked on Donna and Zane's door. She was shown into their rear lounge while Lucifurr, Ross and I watched from the back fence. When she started shouting and pulled the disposable textile-cutting scalpel out of her handbag, Jane and Alf, who had been watching Ermine for days, stepped out from behind the curtains and swiftly disarmed her. Just as I'd planned. The following morning Ermine was charged with Jack McWally's murder.

🐈

It was Sunday morning. Ross and I were lying on the sunny rear porch listening to Jane explain the case to Grace as they sat in the deckchairs.

'Everyone has squawked now, so we know who did what. It was a case of missing gastropods, or rather missing limpets,' she said.

'But how did you know they were missing?' Grace asked.

'We got an anonymous tip-off. A video from Jack's beach of a woman removing limpets and replacing them with dog whelks.'

'But you don't eat dog whelks,' said Grace, 'everyone knows that.'

'That's how we knew Pollock was not involved in it. Like Zane and Donna, he wanted limpets on the rocks. Jack's beach is the only stretch of rocky shore in both directions. Pollock wanted to launch his revolutionary hors d'oeuvre, flame-grilled limpets in garlic butter and samphire, served in a windscreen spray cleaner mist. But he had to have local limpets.'

'Why wouldn't Jack sell him the beach?'

'Because he was funding Donna and Zane, who were trialling a new industry. Something that will give Whitstable a world-famous reputation.'

'OK, what?'

'Do you know what the hardest thing in the natural world is?' said Jane.

'Limpets?'

'No, limpet teeth. Tougher than spider silk. Little gnashers made of something called goethite, encased in protein. Zane had already got form in biomimicry, imitating flying fish aerodynamics for the Pink Balls F1 team. But this was a private project, bankrolled by Jack McWally.'

'Why was he interested?'

Jane took two postcard-sized pictures from her jacket and passed them to Grace. I hopped onto her lap to have a look. The first showed a glum-looking teenage Jack holding up a trophy. The second was the smiling picture I'd seen of him in Jane's file.

'Notice anything?' said Jane.

'Well, in this one he has beautiful teeth,' said Grace, pointing at the second picture.

'As a boy he had brittle teeth and kept having them knocked out in matches. But with those sparklers he could gnaw through oaks. This all began when Zane told him about limpet teeth. Jack agreed to bankroll the project and they set up the Whitstable Teeth Strengthening Company, WTSC Ltd. Jack was the first and only human trial.'

'But how does Regan Ermine fit in?'

'Well, she had used those rocks illegally to farm dog whelks for quite a while. She extracted mucus from the hypobranchial gland on the whelk to make purple dye – known as Tyrian purple. She then dyed the parchments of her sexually explicit illuminated artworks. Her famous *codex purpureum* collection.'

'But why kill Jack?'

'When Jack bought the beach and installed more rocks she thought she was quids in. She borrowed heavily to ramp up to produce the Imperial purple silks and togas increasingly worn by filthy-rich DFLs. When we raided her home we found vats full of putrefying dog whelks.'

'So she used whelks to poison him,' said Grace.

'She seduced him, then discovered his intention to grow millions of limpets. He had to go. And she used poisoned whelks to implicate Pollock, whom she knew also wanted a limpet-only beach.'

'I was coming to Pollock. What did he have on Zane which convinced him that Donna would sell him the beach?' asked Grace.

'Zane has not yet managed to replicate limpet teeth in his lab. He could only produce artificial teeth by cutting off the 1mm-long teeth of thousands of limpets and blending them into human-sized gnashers.'

'How awful.'

'I know. Imagine all those limpets helplessly sliding off rocks. Somehow, Pollock found out and threatened to expose the couple to the whelk protection movement. They would have been cancelled by them as gastropod murderers in no time.'

'So what now?' asked Grace.

'Jack's will leaves his assets to the local football club, including WTSC Ltd. When Zane replicates limpet teeth artificially the club will be richer than Croesus. In a few years we should be playing Barcelona and Juventus at the Montibel ground – probably in a new 60,000 capacity stadium. The team have already decided to change the Whelkies' unofficial club name to The Limpets.'

When Ross and I left, Jane was speculating on the identity of the anonymous sender of the Regan Ermine video. Good luck there, lady. We jumped over the fence to join Lucifurr in the undergrowth around the Crab & Winkle Way. Our overlarge associate had developed a taste for the seaside and was resting after his early morning swim.

'What I don't understand,' he said, 'was how you knew there was something wrong with Pollock being arrested for Jack's murder?'

'It was the picture of Jack's body that proved the murderer knew nothing about football. Pollock is a keen supporter of the Limpets. Ermine is an artist – so say no more.'

Ross and Lucifurr looked at each other in puzzlement.

'Jack's shinguards were on the wrong legs,' I said.

They both nodded at me in admiration. Quite right too.

Later, I pondered on the never-ending cycle of cruel human exploitation and genocide of species useful to them. Dog whelks' glands mashed for filthy porn-art and upmarket Tyrian purple clothing. Limpet teeth sawn off for a better dental appearance. And whelks infused with expensive auto-products and consumed purely to display status. Was there no end to the vanity of *homo sapiens?* I quite like some of them, but they ruin everything.

Still, one superior species with no useful purpose at all to humans still stands atop the evolutionary pyramid. And we'll still be here long after the useless biped is gone.

4

The Limbless Catalytic Burglars

Caper

THREE DAYS AFTER THE GASTROPODS CASE ROSS AND I WERE bundled into our cat carriers by Grace and driven to the vets for our annual check-up. Ross always gets paranoid his time is up and is usually car-sick. He cowers down until he is delivered back home to the safety of his study. I sit in the back seat, watch the trees fly by and wish I could travel the world at such speed all the time. I always think back to my first stay in the vets, after I'd been found in a cardboard shoe box, the runt of the litter ripped away from my mother's warmth and dumped behind some bins.

Ben was contacted by the vet's nurse, who knew he was looking for a kitten, and the rest as they say, was love at first sight. So every visit to a vet reminds me of him and makes me sad. I've sworn to avenge his brutal murder by the Kincaids, but that seems impossible at present. And that hurts a lot more than any injection.

In the vet's car park Grace plonked our carriers on the

ground while we queued outside to be seen, distanced from the other pet owners. I gazed out behind us through the mesh of my carrier at the sad spectacle of local petdom waiting to be treated. The usual selection of overweight under-exercised Whitstable dogs was on show, a Lab straining at its leash and two Yorkies snapping back at it from behind their owner's heels. What a canine shower!

I turned around to the front carrier mesh window and noticed a curiosity in front of us. A bright orange-chested parrot with a white head and rich blue wings, chatting away to all and sundry from its cage. He attracted my interest immediately because he was obviously a far more intelligent animal than any of the other pets present.

He was happily tearing up the egg-box his human had put in the cage, and occasionally looking up to sing to the harassed pet-owners in the queue.

Oh when the Spurs, go marching in.
Oh when the Spurs go marching in,
I wanna be in that number,
When the Spurs go marching in.

At least that raised a smile or two, that is until he moved on to his next set of verbals. Which was repeatedly delivered in a squeal of fear.

What the f*** is that coming over the house!
It nearly took the bleeding roof off.

I waited for the humorous football punchline before I realised there wasn't one.

'Sorry about the language,' said the owner, a flat-capped beardie in his 50s, looking round at Grace.

'Who was he imitating?' Grace said.

'Err, me actually. Something flew down our street a few nights ago, about 2am. Scared the cr— scared the hell out of me.'

'Where was this?' asked Grace.

'Station Road. I ran out, and there were neighbours outside in their jim-jams in the street looking up, but whatever it was had gone south towards the station. Some idiot with an oversized drone having a laugh I shouldn't wonder.'

At that moment, the vet popped his head out of the door.

'Mr de Bergerac and Beaky?'

And our man was off, with Beaky now loudly cawing that Arsenal were shite. Beautiful and clever, I surmised.

Oversized drone my posterior, though. I looked across at Ross in his case and he shook his head quickly in agreement. Quite – a little mystery here, but not a crime, so sadly we'd have to let it go. But one for his data bank.

We were pronounced as fit as the proverbial fiddles and driven home post-haste. As Grace was unloading us from the car, Ross whispered out of the side of his mouth.

'Watch out, here come Napoleon and his sidekick,' he said.

'Damn,' I replied.

Indeed, we were being determinedly marched upon by Des Cart, the local Neighbourhood Watch coordinator, and the deputy, his American wife, Dusty. They had recently taken over the role from Grace, who had done it sensibly for years, and practically militarised it. But there was no escape and I saw Grace's shoulders sag as they reached us.

'Hi there, stranger,' said Dusty in a Southern drawl. Somehow, with her TV-presenter bleached hair and steely grey eyes, she managed to make it sound vaguely intimidating.

'Hello, lovely to see you too,' said Grace, summoning a smile from the deepest recesses of her soul.

Des knelt down to peer in the carriers. He examined Ross and me carefully in turn, as if we were crime scene artefacts.

'Annual check-up, heh,' he said.

Bloody hell, I thought. Say hello to CSI Whitstable.

'That's right. Must get them in. They will be starving, or bursting,' Grace laughed.

'This won't take a moment, little lady,' said Dusty, 'and it will be especially interesting to you with your police... connections.'

She winked as she said it. I would have given up my salmon treats forever to throw up on her trainers at that moment.

'Yes, it's great to live in such a diverse neighbourhood,' echoed Des.

Make that two sets of trainers.

There was a long awkward silence before he piped up again.

'Right. Anyway, the reason we are making the rounds is to let people know about the epidemic of catalytic converter robberies in the neighbourhood,' he said.

'Epidemic?' said Grace.

'Yes, honey, it's really serious,' said Dusty, 'It's the biggest crime wave we've had here for years. And it's not just cars and vans. Local garages have been broken into as well. Do you have a cat clamper?'

Grace looked down at us in alarm.

'A cat clamper? No, why?'

'No. a catalytic clamper. You can fix it to your exhaust pipes. Makes it really tough to steal the catalytic converter,' said Des.

'Oh, right. Well, I'll certainly look into it.'

'You do that, sweetie. And tell that gorgeous girlfriend of yours we are doing everything we can to help her beat this crimewave and protect the public,' said Dusty.

OK, this is getting weird now, I thought. Get us the hell indoors, Grace. We've finally got a crime to solve.

🐈

Our first step was to start collecting information on this spate of catalytic converter robberies. The following morning, after Grace and Jane had left for work, Ross powered up the desktop and perused the cesspit of misinformation known as the Internet while I combed through the local free rags. On Grace's iPad I also looked through the increasingly hysterical emails she'd received and ignored from Des and Dusty Cart over the previous days.

There's a fine line between informing and warning people and scaring the shit out of them. The Carts were so far over it that they'd reached Paranoiaville.

To prevent catalytic converter theft, Grace was expected to do pretty much everything up to and including welding herself to the underside of the car holding an automatic assault weapon. And I wasn't even sure her ancient Volvo estate *had* a catalytic converter. The cat clamper alone was a wimpy token effort as far as the Carts were concerned.

It was also clear from the emails that the Carts had much more detailed information from the police on the dates and places of the robberies than they were sharing. Since Grace's police detective lover Jane Austenson was unlikely to provide us with what we needed we'd have to get it direct.

Time for a black op, I said to myself.

Later, Ross and I compared notes over lunch.

'Do the Carts have a pet?' I asked him.

Ross looked away. When he turned back his eyes looked empty and defeated.

'They had a female Persian at one time, called Golf,' he said.

'Golf?'

'Yes, you know, golf... cart.'

'Hysterical. What happened to her?'

'Dusty Cart drives their bloody oversized jeep like a maniac. She accidentally ran Golf over while she was sleeping in their drive.'

'That's terrible.'

Not the first American to drive over a local resident without sanction, I thought. But Ross was more charitable.

'All humans are careless. You know that. Hopefully it was over quickly.'

I'd never seen him so miserable. I tried to change the subject.

'What about a dog?'

'They had a German shepherd, called Go.'

'Christ, what humans do to their pets. You said "had". Where is he now?'

'He took the hint and went. Living happily in Brighton now, I believe, called Ranger.'

'Hmm. So they have a cat-flap?'

'Yes, but the house is full of cameras and alarms. We'll have to be really careful not to be rumbled.'

'So you know the layout?'

'Yes, pretty well. I can sketch it out.'

I could imagine how he'd acquired the knowledge, but males will be males, even a blancmange like Ross.

'Good,' I said. 'But we'll need some muscle to help us get in and out. Get Lucifurr over here tomorrow, same time. Anything else?' I asked.

'Well, the crime spree is not limited to catalytic converters. As Dusty said, there's all sorts of thieving going on in town. Tools, electrics, even steel sheets.'

'Some sort of engineering project?' I said.

'It certainly looks like it's all being nicked to order,' he answered.

'OK, we'll have a better idea about that when we get hold of these crime reports.'

Ross nodded and sloped off, still looking miserable. It's difficult to remember sometimes that there are a million stories in this dirty old town and most of them have grim endings.

The following lunchtime found the three of us sitting on Grace's desk in the study poring (we call it pawing) over the details of our caper. We examined the floor plan of the Cart house that Ross had drawn on the iPad while he pointed out the key features.

'We've scouted the outside of the house. The only entry

has to be through the rear cat-flap. It's a locked brown and white Safeflap model 23 with 9, 10 and 15 microchip security, with 4 AA batteries which are probably still live. Have your come across this one before, Lucifurr?' Ross asked.

'Sure. Piece of piss. If it's locked in the exit only position as you remember, the flap has a 3mm give when pressed. Enough to hook one of these babies around and lift.'

He held out his fearsome right paw's razor-sharp claws.

'OK,' said Ross. 'Inside, we have to hug the right wall to avoid the automated alarm digicams here and here.'

As he spoke he pawed a USB stick around the iPad's surface to represent our progress through the house. Lucifurr and I nodded sagely.

'Then we have a closed door at the end of the corridor leading to the study.'

'No worries,' said Lucifurr.

'What do you mean, no worries? How do we open it?' I said.

'Standard door handles right, Ross?' said Lucifurr.

'Yes, I think so...'

'Don't think, Ross, you've got to know,' I said, feeling my fur rising in irritation.

'OK, OK, let me think.'

He scratched his left ear while he tried to remember. My tail tapped the desk top with increasing force.

Yes, I'm sure, dammit,' he said at last.

'No sweat then,' said Lucifurr, 'what's behind the door?'

'A corridor that runs left and right. You turn left and the second door on the right is the study. That's where their Neighbourhood Watch stuff is kept.'

'How long have we got?' said Lucifurr.

'Like all humans they are creatures of stupid habits. They work from home but Des goes for his barefoot run at 10.00am. Dusty returns from her distanced Krav Maga class at 10.20,' I said.

We looked at each other. Lucifurr struck out his paw and pinged the USB across the room.

'Shit. It's really tight,' he growled.

'We *do* need longer,' I said, 'at least a couple more minutes.'

'If she comes back and finds us, we are stuffed,' said Ross. He pressed the home button on the iPad and the floor plan disappeared.

I looked at him.

'Unless... it's OK, I have an idea,' I said, 'but you won't like it.'

'Why?'

'Because you won't be inside with us.'

'What? But I know the layout!'

'You are too emotionally involved. And now we know the layout as well. Anyway, it's your fault.'

'My fault?'

'Yes, you're the only eye candy on the team.'

🐈

That evening I curled up on Grace's lap feigning affection while she held hands with Jane on the sofa and they watched the first episode of some vast box set they'd just started. Ross lay on his back on the carpet watching it upside down as usual. We put on a show like this regularly just to listen to any juicy crime morsels Jane might share. On screen, a planet was being nuked by aliens and the humans were being fried in their millions. That's why I love sci-fi – it's such an emotional catharsis.

'So how was work?' said Grace.

'Oh, you know, busy. We are a bit stretched now that Whitstable has become the burglary capital of Kent overnight.'

'Really?' said Jane.

My ears had pricked up but I forced myself to focus on the screen. The surviving humans had set off in their spaceships to find a new home planet. The aliens were after them, chewing their fleeing craft up one by one like nibbling crisps out of a packet. This stuff was really good but I zoned out of it to focus on what Jane was saying.

'Yes,' she said, 'some professional outfit is raiding local engineering and electrical businesses for their tools, stock and what-not. All high-end gear and materials. And now there's also a separate spate of home burglaries and plant robberies going on. Weird stuff – frozen fish nicked from a garage freezer, root vegetables dug out of allotments, even a tea caddy from a kitchen, along with the plug-in kettle.'

'So you're a domestic appliance detective now?' said Grace.

'No, funny girl, I'm investigating the theft from the businesses and the chopped-off arm we found.'

Grace gasped and I dug my claws into her jeans to stop her jumping up.

'Ouch, bad girl, Flic,' she said, rubbing her thighs down, 'what chopped-off arm?'

'We found a male left hand and a bit of its arm on the floor of Thompson's Tools after the last robbery, next to where a stolen cordless metal saw was attached to a work bench.

Someone got careless detaching it, we think.'

'Good God,' said Grace.

Then after a moment she spoke again.

'Were the fingerprints known to you?'

Jane laughed.

'You're all heart, Grace. No, but I think the thieves might be taking a break for a bit as there's been nothing for a day or so. And nothing has been reported from local hospitals either. Which gives us more time to deal with your nosy neighbours.'

'You don't mean Des and Dusty?'

'I do mean them. They've started an anti-burglary patrol every night, from 10pm to 3am. A sort of masked sub-vigilante "Save our vegetables and kettles" group. They are scaring the crap out of anyone looking outside when they close their curtains for the night. We get the terrified calls and have to send cars out to calm the public.'

'They've not asked me to join in,' said Grace.

Jane leaned over to kiss Grace.

'They know you've got more sense. Still, I wish you were still in charge.'

On screen the credits were rolling. The human ships had narrowly survived a shuddering space battle and hyper-jumped away to postpone their extinction. Shame.

I jumped off Grace's lap and headed upstairs to my basket. As Philip K. Dick once said, if you think this Universe is bad, you should see some of the others.

The church clock struck 10am and a moment later we heard the Cart front door slam.

'Now,' I said to Lucifurr.

We jumped out from behind the buddleia bush and set to work. Lucifurr sat outside the cat-flap and pressed it hard with his left paw while I laid Grace's tiny action camera on the step to rest my jaws for a bit. Lucifurr slowly worked one of his right claws into the tiny gap he'd created. After a couple of nerve-wracking minutes he suddenly flipped up the flap and darted his head forward to wedge it in the space. The flap came to rest on his shoulders.

'Good work,' I said.

'Brawn before brains,' he answered, slipping through the flap, but leaving his tail to wedge the flap ajar.

I picked up the cam and wormed myself around the flap, my snout to his arse. Inside, we squeezed along on the right-hand side of the corridor until we reached the door at the end. I looked up and sighed in relief. It sported a standard polished brass curled Georgian handle on a matching backplate. Lucifurr didn't hang about. Or rather he did, leaping up to hang off the handle with his right paw while his left curled around the edge of the door. The handle lowered and he worked his claws into the gap. A few seconds later we were peeping around the door into the corridor. Nothing stirred. We edged along to the study door which had the same handle model. Lucifurr repeated the trick and in a trice we were in our treasure cave.

It was unlike any study I'd ever seen in the neighbourhood. Opposite, there was an enormous map of the town facing us from the far wall but the room was dominated by a large square table lit by overhanging snooker lights. I leapt up onto the corner of it and found myself gazing down on a 3-D relief map of Whitstable, Seasalter and Tankerton. Almost every street was carefully reconstructed. Here was the Ancient Poseidon by the beach, there was the Duke of Cumbria, close to the Whitstable Whelk Company's restaurant The Swearbox, each model a thing of beauty. And scattered across the map were a series of red cubes, each with a tiny annotated flag. The flag on the cube next to Thomson's Tools carried the legend 'Power and Cutting gear.' The dozen other red cubes were carefully positioned outside other engineering, electronic and electrical retailers. I switched on the cam and started photographing all the different crime locations on the map.

'Look at this,' said Lucifurr when I'd finished.

I looked up at him with the cam still in my mouth. He was gazing at the map on the far wall. I turned off the cam and walked on the ocean side of the map until I reached him.

The map was covered with blue pins displaying the recent house and shed burglaries. These were taking place further inland, where the allotments and residential properties were. Something was stirring in me. I switched on the action cam and adjusted the ISO and exposure compensation for the poor light, then shot each crime spot carefully.

'Time to go, Flic,' said Lucifurr.

I looked up at the round wall clock behind us. It read 10.19am. I jumped onto the small desk under the wall map and glanced at the notes scribbled on a loose-leaf pad. At the bottom, the words '*Combine the results?*' in red ink leapt out.

'Come on, Flic,' hissed Lucifurr.

We jumped down and rushed to the open door.

But we were already too late. As we edged out of the room we looked back down the corridor and froze in terror. At the far end we could see the dark shape of the returning Dusty's head through the frosted window of the front door. The key

81

was being turned in the lock. In a moment she would step inside and spot us.

'Back,' hissed Lucifurr.

'Wait,' I said.

We heard Ross's miaowing in the next instant. He really laid it on, the little trollop. No doubt winding in and out between her calves and lying on his back exposing his fluffy white stomach to her. But it had the desired effect immediately.

'Oh, you little darling,' I heard her say, 'are you lost, Rossy?'

Dusty's head shape at the window disappeared as she bent down to stroke him.

'Now!' I said.

In an instant we were through the next door and at the cat-flap, pushing through and diving into the buddleia. We watched from behind its leaves as Dusty appeared at the kitchen window moments later, looking out into the garden as she downed her energy drink.

'Let's get out of here,' I said when she disappeared.

The three of us reconvened at our spot in the Crab & Winkle Way undergrowth. Ross was already there, licking himself down. He looked up at us.

'Successful mission?' he asked.

I dropped the action cam at his paws.

'All there,' I said.

'Good, but don't ever make me do that with that woman ever again. I've never felt so dirty.'

It was a while before Lucifurr and I stopped rolling around laughing.

Ross showed us the result of his analysis that afternoon on Grace's desktop. He had plotted the crime points on the Carts' table onto an Ordnance Survey map but had not identified any obvious common factors. The same was true of the burglary points on the wall map.

'The Carts initially assumed that the two crime waves were unrelated due to their nature,' he said.

'But they have now twigged,' I said.

'Yes, the thieves are stealing engineering items but also having to nick food and drink because they are stuck here.'

'Well, we know one of them has lost a hand,' said Lucifurr.

'Sure, that might restrict them, but strangely no medication has been burgled,' said Ross.

'Anyway,' he continued, 'I combined the crime details and applied median centre spatial analysis to the data using a highly-clustered index of dispersion.'

He clicked forward to the next slide of his dynamic presentation. The blue and red crime points appeared on a single map, following North-South and East-West axes which divided the total crime points either side of each line in two. Then the map expanded around the cross-hairs of the compass lines.

'Zooming in,' he said, 'we see that the median centre of this crime wave is...'

'...the old empty dairy building next to the railway line,' said Lucifurr.

'Exactly,' said Ross.

'Great hideout for a Whitstable gang, and only a few hundred yards from us,' I said.

'This analysis is relatively easy. The Carts are going to work it out very quickly,' said Ross.

I agreed with him – it wasn't rocket science. Once the Carts solved this crime-spree they would become truly unbearable. Time to take out the competition.

'Well, let's make sure we get in there first then,' I said. 'Just one question, Ross,'

'Yes?'

'Why nick catalytic converters?'

'For the palladium and rhodium. The palladium is used in fuel cells, and reacts with hydrogen to make electricity, heat and water. The rhodium can be combined to resist high temperature. It's also brilliant so it's used as a jewellery finish.'

It was starting to come together in my mind.

It was nearly midnight and the three of us were sitting in the overgrown bushes in the back yard of the old dairy. It was another cloudless night, the moon a slim curled sliver above us. We'd scouted the front earlier but there was no obvious entry point. The building was a rectangular block of pale brick of 1920s vintage with a high roof and barn-style faded wooden doors, winged by small two-storey offices with boarded-up windows. At the front, a wide tarmac drive had once allowed the milk wagons to be loaded off the main road.

The windows at the front of the dairy were also covered on the inside with plastic bags so that no light emerged. But at the rear, which backed onto a small copse, our criminal elements had been less careful. Between the planks of the boarded up windows we could see shards of light from within.

We were still cogitating how to enter the building when the rear door opened and a young woman in an over-sized face mask wearing workman's gloves emerged carrying a collection of steel pipes and pieces of sheet metal in her arms. She wore a tight-fitting but battered khaki uniform. She walked past us and carefully concealed her haul under the lush undergrowth close to the trees. As she walked back she hesitated for a moment as she passed us. Then she made three more trips, carrying more materials, tools and a plug-in kettle before disappearing back into dairy, leaving the door open.

'It's a trap,' said Ross.

'She can't possibly have seen us in this darkness,' said Lucifurr.

'We have to take a look,' I said.

We edged up to the doorway and I peered around.

'Come in, friends,' said a woman's voice.

We looked at each other and crept in. She was leaning against the wall of the dairy hall, which was spotless. Next to her stood a man in an identical uniform. They both wore the same large masks but I could see they had delicate smooth faces and fine short hair. I would have taken them for brother and sister. His left arm was bandaged and the hand encased in an industrial glove with the fingers and thumb flopping down. In his right hand he held a steaming mug which he raised to us, round eyes creased in a smile. In the far corner, a slim arched structure about the size of an SUV had been concealed beneath an ancient green tarpaulin.

'I'm Sylk and he's Nilon. We are just cleaning up before we leave,' said the woman.

You'd better get a move on then, I thought. Chances are the local Keystone vigilantes will be here with their cricket bats soon.

'Yes, we know,' said the man. 'We had to crash-land and

repair after getting hit by some human space-junk orbiting your planet. Everything works again but we just need a couple of hours to adjust our jump-drive and then we'll be out of your fur.'

I felt every strand of fur on my body stretch out in terror. I looked around at Ross and Lucifurr. We all looked like hairy puffer fish.

'Don't scare them, Nilon,' said Sylk.

'Yes, sorry Flic. We're telepaths, of course. And Lucifurr, don't worry about my hand, mate,' said Nilon.

He withdrew his arm from the glove and unwrapped the bandage. At the end of the stump, tiny fingers and thumbs had formed. He looked across at Ross, who had also not spoken.

'Yes, you are right, It's just like your Axolotl salamanders. We form a blastema and then the cells re-differentiate and the limb reforms. We cracked the code for limb regeneration eons ago – one of our many gene-splicing tricks. You see, we are always losing bits of ourselves on our travels,' he said, glancing at Sylk.

Sylk answered my next thought question.

'Earth, of course, Flic. Isn't any planet "Earth" to those who live on it?'

There was a sudden rapping on the front doors of the dairy. I immediately recognised Des Cart's less than dulcet tones.

'Hallo, who's in there?' he barked.

'Surrender. We've called the feds,' added Dusty unhelpfully.

'Shut up, Dusty – it's not the f****** OK Corral,' shouted Des.

The exchange was followed by more banging by the two of them on the aged doors.

Sylk looked at me and frowned.

'No, unfortunately we can't vaporise them. This is a peaceful mission. Any ideas where we could hide out?' she said.

'We have a place nearby you can sit it out for a couple of hours,' I thought-said, 'but how can you get that thing out of here unnoticed?'

Nilon and Sylk pointed upwards. I looked up at great gap in the roof and the stars swirling above it.

'Made it yesterday. More than enough space to get her out,' said Nilon.

He put his cup down on the window ledge and pulled away the cracked tarpaulin to reveal the most beautiful shiny object I'd ever seen.

'Well, let's be off quick then,' I thought-said.

🐈

It was almost dusk and Jane was telling Grace about the local disturbance the previous evening as they sat outside. From the lounge, the lovely sounds of Sun Ra's Arkestra spilled into the garden. Music of a guy who'd been to Saturn.

'We were called out about 1am by the neighbours. Des and Dusty Cart were banging on the doors and windows of the old dairy with their garden utensils, shouting at the supposed criminals to come out.'

'Good God – the poor neighbours. What did you do?' said Grace.

'We tried to reason with them, but they kept screaming that they had proof the dairy was the epicentre of Whitstable's criminal community and that they'd just flown off in a silver UFO. Dusty then started screaming that it was Roswell all over again so we agreed to open up the place to prove there was no one there. But they still didn't accept it, so in the end we had to put both of them in the cells for the night. Grade-A nut-jobs, both of them.'

'Poor Des and Dusty,' said Grace. 'They'll have to resign from Neighbourhood Watch for sure.'

'We'll make bloody certain of it. We can't have them whipping up the neighbours like this.'

'I guess I'll have to pick up the coordinator job again,' said Grace wistfully.

'Absolutely,' said Jane downing her glass.

That's all I wanted to hear. We'd be able to read all the local crime reports again without having to break into some other weirdo's place. I looked over at Ross and we crept away over the garden to our clearing in the Crab & Winkle Way, or Cape Cataveral as we now called it. It was a clear July night and Ross was giving me and Lucifurr a short lecture on Jupiter later. Then we'd head up towards one of the fields above Whelkville, where we'd lie on our backs trying to spot the planet among the stars, still processing what had happened to us.

They'd loaded us quickly into the cockpit of the spaceship, then strapped themselves in and switched on its silent anti-gravity thruster. The silvered craft had lifted itself above the old dairy and floated low over the trees while we guided it to our clearing. My mind had been exploding with questions throughout.

'What are you doing here?' I'd thought-said.

'Checking on your advance, where you are on the IoB,'

replied Sylk.

'IoB?'

'Index of Barbarity, which determines when you can be admitted to the civilised galaxy. You were getting closer in the 1960s and early 70s, but you've slipped back.'

'Yes, preliminary calculations suggest you are now at 5 in your Earth years,' said Nilon.

'Only 5 years!!' I said.

They burst out laughing.

'No – only 5,000 years, Flic,' said Sylk.

We'd descended into the clearing and they'd placed the three of us gently on *terra firma*, as if that really exists. A few hours later, shortly before dawn, Lucifurr, Ross and I sat on our garden paving and watched the gorgeous claw-shaped vessel raise itself smoothly above the trees. Even the red logo of the Whitstable Sheet Metal Co. on its side did not detract from its grace. It rose up silently inside some invisible lift shaft until it was but a silver pinprick in the darkness. Then with a sudden spark it was gone, having hyper-jumped deep into the cosmos.

I thought then of Sylk's last words to me as she said goodbye.

'Never let your morals stop you doing the right thing, Flic,' she said.

'Hang on – isn't that a quote from Isaac Asimov?' I'd thought-asked.

She'd laughed then, taking off her mask to show her beautiful incisors and rough pink tongue, her long graceful whiskers twitching as she chuckled.

'Yes, busted,' she said.

5

The Theoretical Whitstable

Postcard Fetishisation Case

A FTER THE LIMBLESS CATALYTIC BURGLARS CASE WE HAD A long quiet patch in the last few weeks of July and I found myself increasingly tetchy and depressed. I told myself it was just the endless pandemic but I dressed it up in intellectual bollocks. 'Now is the time of monsters,' I'd mutter to Lucifurr darkly, 'the old world dying and the new struggling to be born.' He'd give me a blank look and carry on crunching down on yet another poor still-squirming mouse on top of Cape Cataveral. Not that Lucifurr's own hegemony was under threat, as he lorded it over a local empire of Mongol proportions, but it made me feel a bit better. And he actually liked the monster tag too. In reality, while I was worried about Jane and Grace getting the virus, I was also directionless without a live meaty case of my own.

The vacuum of the times had affected Ross in a different way. The pandemic had made him turn his back on his feline bourgeois existence and he had fallen prey to the allure of Situationism, an ideology to which cats are particularly susceptible. Having always been a bit of a *flaneur,* he now adopted the more radical strategy of *derivé,* letting himself drift through the psychogeography of Whelkville to encounter new experiences and situations that would enhance his reality. I was sure the most likely experience he'd have would be a sudden close encounter with the wheel of a Jeep Cherokee, but arguing with him was pointless. When I eventually told him to get a grip he gave me a studied gallic shrug.

'You really need to pursue your authentic desires and free yourself from the capitalist spectacle of commodification, Flic,' he said.

'Christ – just eat your nice expensive biscuits and piss off to your comfy pillow,' I replied.

'*Sous les pavés, la plage,*' he muttered as he turned away, crushed by my wit.

What the f*** does that mean, I thought. But having myself once been an adept of the sacred texts of the Situationist International I knew it was not that easy. What we really needed was a decent case quickly.

But Fate is a cruel, smiling, card-dealing trickster and she now turned over her joker. The following afternoon Grace returned in a daze from an end-of-first-lockdown sourdough loaf-making course at the newly established Whitstable bijou baker Cereal & Fender. She walked into the lounge and poured herself a half-pint of malt whisky before slumping onto the sofa and bursting into tears. She was still sobbing quietly when Jane came in from work and found her.

'What on earth has happened?' she said.

'They're here,' said Grace.

'Who's here?'

'The Kincaids have come to take over the town.'

It took a while for Jane to get the full story. Grace had turned up at her class along with the other student bakers to be met by a smiling, curly-haired, tattooed and bearded thirty-something guy called Billy. He'd quickly charmed the pants off them all with his hackneyed mockney spiel. Then he'd introduced his small and doubtless underpaid baking team before leaving on some urgent errand. Something about him had jarred but it wasn't until she was making the knife slash down the middle of the dough that she experienced the moment of terror when her slow-acting memory banks finally made the match. Of course – he'd introduced himself as Billy. Take off the hair and beard and lose the patter and you were left with Billy Kincaid, prime enforcer of the gang and heir-apparent of the clan.

Over lunch Grace got the rest of the story from Albertina, the shaggy-haired and dungareed team leader on the course. The Kincaid family were lovely and so on trend. As well as Cereal & Fender they'd taken over the renamed Fearsome Arms and also bought out a number of the arty shops near the harbour. She knew they were also now in discussions to take over the Chattels art gallery in Oxford Street following the very unfortunate fire which had ruined the owner a month earlier.

Grace had quietly sipped her latte and pitied the smooth-faced ingenue as she'd prattled on about how wonderful it was that the Kincaid family cared so much about the culture of Whitstable.

'Don't overdo it, Albertina love,' said a voice behind her.

Grace had looked around and up into the face of Billy Kincaid, who'd returned unannounced to check on the course's progress. Only now his dark eyes were much harder and did not match his fixed smile. He held the list of participants in his hand.

'Grace, is it,' he'd said, 'Grace Johns?'

In terror, she'd stumbled over the reply. Yes, that's right, she'd muttered. Then he'd sat down and fired his own questions at her, his tone nevertheless remaining smooth caramel. By the time the class had resumed she was a train wreck, wondering how much she'd revealed of herself. She'd slept-walked through the afternoon and her sourdough creation had emerged from the oven looking like a meteorite-scoured elephant turd. Her description not mine.

'Don't worry, Grace. Believe me, things could be a very great deal worse,' Billy had whispered to her, leaning in close.

The words had entered her like a jagged-edged blade. She'd fled from the bakery as soon as the course had ended, dumping the pitted loaf in the nearest bin. Now she sat leaning forward, her elbows on her knees, weeping bitterly while Jane stroked her back.

'Don't worry,' Jane said, 'I'll make sure that nothing bad happens.'

Grace looked up at Jane.

'You have no idea what this lot are like. They execute coppers for fun – you have to be really careful as well.'

I watched them hug each other tightly. The two humans who together with Ross were the only beings I could call family were now in danger. I felt the fur on my tail puff out at the thought of any of them being hurt and a hot fury coursed through me. Not on my watch, I swore.

Later that afternoon I brought Ross and Lucifurr up to speed with Grace's close encounter with Billy Kincaid. We agreed it was too dangerous at present to approach the Rottweiler-guarded Kincaid lair in Tankerton. But just in case they made an appearance at Grace's, Lucifurr agreed to mount a security detail around the house over the next few nights. Meanwhile, Ross and I would investigate the business activities of the family since their relocation to our seaside haven.

Our online research on Grace's iPad confirmed the information Grace had gleaned from Albertina. We first investigated 'Pop' Kincaid, failed abstract artist and self-styled gastro-entrepreneur. He had purchased the Fearsome Arms near the sea-front just before lockdown and had turned it into an 'art celebration of all things Whitstable while you fill your face,' according to the local paper. His own bald, spherical head certainly did a good job of filling the photo that accompanied the article. Did anyone really wear jewelled ear studs in this day and age?

With the relaxing of restrictions, he'd been coining it as DFLs with more money than sense snapped up oversaturated sunset seascapes as they gobbled their desserts. With his impending purchase of Chattels he would shortly hold a monopoly of the local high-end art market.

Meanwhile, super-woke ex-cage fighter and master baker Billy was also running the local souvenir shop empire. His 'buy three postcards and get a free Whitstabun at Cereal & Fender' special offer was killing the other postcard sellers.

94

For visitors without the funds or with too much sense to buy an overpriced painting or print in the Fearsome Arms or Chattels, Billy was rapidly turning into the only provider of a physical printed memory of their day out at the seaside.

As far as we could see from scanning the back issues, burlesque artist and rap DJ 'Wild Hog' Fenella, the matriarch and brains of the Kincaid operation, was still residing in Stoke Newington. She only came down to be photographed popping out of her leather-bondage gear when the Kincaids executed a new local business coup.

When Ross and I had concluded our online research we sat back and looked at each other.

'What they are doing is distasteful,' he said, 'but I doubt if it's criminal.'

'Why not – they are restricting competition,' I said.

'How so? They are not stopping other people opening an art gallery here or selling postcards in their local shop.'

I slammed the desk with my tail.

'You know these bastards are up to no good,' I growled.

Ross's ears twitched in sympathy.

'OK – I'll see what else I can dig up on their business dealings. It may take a while,' he said.

'Good – meanwhile, I'll see what else they might be doing to control the local crime scene,' I said.

I was glad to have given Ross something to get his teeth into. With luck, it would keep him clear of the seductive intellectual comforts of Situationism, which was rather like Sherlock Holmes turning to the needle between cases.

I'd also asked Lucifurr, the muscle of our crime-busting operation, to keep an eye on Ross while he went through his ideological mid-life crisis. Finding himself at a loose end, he had been following Ross at a discreet distance on his random wanderings through the town to make sure our *chat-savant* didn't get himself in trouble. Little did I know that Ross would spot him and quickly inveigle him into his ideological web. So it was a surprise when they both turned up the following lunchtime, looking rather full of themselves.

'We've found it,' said Lucifurr.

I looked up from the Elmore Leonard I was re-reading on Grace's Kindle account. Pure genius dialogue, perfect for taking my mind off the Grace situation.

'Found who – Shergar?'

'The Kincaids' secret lair,' said Ross.

'What? How?'

'How? Well, I was observing the reified spectacle of the alienation we call town planning down towards Seasalter when...'

I hissed at him.

'Oh, for f***'s sake, Ross, can it. Lucifurr, what happened?'

'Well, Ross has got a point. The geometry of capitalist construction is like living under a total curfew. Only with the liberation of space can we release the energy to transcend...'

'Oh Christ, not you too,' I shouted, 'I'm so glad we have these little chats but *I know* all this shit. Even Debord acknowledges that unitary urbanism, that is, the total unification of our working and social environment, is a pipe dream at present. At this socio-economic juncture, we therefore accept the permanence of contemporary society and extend our fields of play through experiment with architecture.'

Lucifurr was suitably shocked and looked towards Ross.

'Yeah, she's right,' Ross mumbled.

'So what happened?' I said.

Lucifurr piped up.

'We were trying to protest against a new property in Seasalter which blocks off another bit of the sea view. We were going to register our own special dirty graffiti.'

I sighed.

'You mean you were going to take your usual dump on the front door mat then wait for someone to step in it – pure political infantilism.'

'Maybe. But this bloke did precisely that without noticing and carried it indoors. So we jumped up on the sill to look in and have a good laugh. That's when we saw 'Pop' Kincaid...'

'Sure it was him?'

'Of course, with a young bearded guy,' said Ross.

'But there was someone else being held there,' said Lucifurr.

'Who?'

'Well, it was very odd. First the two of them put on balaclavas and then they brought in a very old man and sat him at a desk.'

'Odd that we know nothing about a kidnapping,' I said.

'It was a pretty weird set-up. The desk was covered in painting materials and drawing paper, and both the masked guys kept shouting at the old man that he had to sketch. That is, until they got a whiff of you know what. That's when we scarpered.'

They both miaowed in pleasure as I pondered their prankish report. Who was this unknown man? What were they forcing him to draw? This was something I had to see. I smiled over at my gang.

'OK – suit up for tonight,' I said, 'it seems we're *back* in the game.'

It was after midnight when Ross and I arrived at Krayfish House, the modernist monstrosity in Seasalter where the victim was being held. Lucifurr was waiting under the low hedge in front of the house. It was a warm July night, and a thunderstorm was brewing out in the estuary. We sprang lightly across the concrete slabs of the front garden and flattened ourselves against the front wall. We each hopped onto one of the large steel cube planters distributed along its length and raised ourselves to peek in through the half-closed vertical blinds into the lounge. Fortunately, one of the tilt-and-turn arch windows was ajar, so we could hear the discussion.

Inside, I could see the masked Pop Kincaid and the young man I presumed to be his son Billy from Grace's description standing behind an impossibly elderly man who was laboriously sketching at the desk. They were barking instructions at the old man on what to draw.

'So in this one we have the old local guy walking his cute terrier along the beach. Two obviously fascist guys are throwing stones at the dog,' Billy was saying.

'This is not really the stuff I used to draw. So how do I represent the young guys as fascists?' asked the old man, as his pencil moved slowly over the paper.

'Come on, Dongal, evolve to a higher plane. You know. Anyone with short hair, no beard and cheap, short-sleeved

98

Red Berry shirt,' answered Pop.

'Err, OK, sorry. And what is your Whittywoke Man doing in this one?'

'You'll love this, Dongal,' said Billy, 'he's standing in the foreground videoing the encounter. The overarching caption above reads, 'Analyse, Agonise, Publicise.''

'Shouldn't he be intervening somehow?'

'Intervene? How is he not intervening – what he's filming is bound to go viral,' said Billy.

'Different in my day,' mumbled the old man, 'we'd go down to Brick Lane and give them what for. Mind you, those were proper fascists.'

Billy and Pop looked at each other and shook their heads in disbelief.

'You'll get there, Dongal,' said Pop.

Dongal? Something was stirring at the back of my mind. I glanced at a pinboard at the side of the room with a number of draft sketches pinned to it. The caricatures were fantastically expressive, the colours vibrant and saturated to excess. Of course! Dongal McDill, the saucy seaside postcard artist, only recently elevated to his proper place in the artistic pantheon. But he must be ancient!

Pop moved across to point at one of the sketches.

'This is a masterpiece, though, Billy,' he said.

'For God's sake, shut your trap – stop using our names,' said Billy.

'Sorry, slipped out,' said Pop.

I looked at the sketch. In the background, against a pale purple sunset, the Ancient Poseidon pub by the beach was engulfed in flames, customers with their clothes on fire jumping out of every possible opening and streaming in terror back into the town. In the left foreground, a smirking Whittywoke Man sat on an outside bench table looking out of the image, a burger and chips untouched by his elbow. The speech bubble stated, 'I only said to the waitress – serving gluten has unfortunate consequences.'

'Yes, that came to me in a detox trance,' said Billy.

'And it's great that you so have raised consciousness, and "turned" Dongal as well – he is really redeeming himself from those appalling art crimes he committed in the 60s,' said Pop.

'You haven't "turned" me – you've kidnapped me! I was perfectly happy eking out my final years in this town!' cried Dongal.

This was more than I could stomach. Plus it was starting to rain. I dropped down into the planter and signalled to the others to fall back to the hedge. We sat under its cover as the rain gathered strength.

'Isn't the old man...' said Ross.

'Yes, Dongal McDill. I had no idea he'd retired to Whelkville.'

'We've got to alert the police,' said Lucifurr.

'Yes, but they're not going to hurt him while he's drawing them new cards. His distinctive style is a goldmine for them. With it they'll be able to drive every other postcard seller in Whelkville out of business.'

What I wasn't saying was that I wanted to bag the whole damn clan, Billy, Pop and 'Wild Hog' Fenella. Two out of three was not good enough and I was sure they were up to more art crime. If they were rigging the blazing sunsets painting scene and kidnapping nonagenarians to try to overwhelm the ironically woke postcard market, then there were clearly no limits.

Ross and Lucifurr looked unconvinced, no doubt thinking I was too close to the case to think straight. But there was no time to debate the matter. The rain had turned to a torrent and our fur coats had already been flattened by the downpour. So we trudged home in bedraggled silence beside the railway track until we reached the edge of Whelkville, then slowly up the hill through the empty backstreets between the darkened houses. Finally, we crossed the sodden graveyard, past the ancient headstones indifferent as to whether lives were spent for good or ill. I realised then that any revenge for Ben's death would be small measure against the loss I felt.

When we at last reached home Lucifurr melted into the darkness on his nightly hunt and Ross and I stumbled through the cat flap. Inside, the lounge was warm and the sofa soft and welcoming. I settled into the hollow where Grace sits and slowly licked my paws clean. A great weariness had enveloped me and carried me into a trance-like state. My eyes closed against my will and I felt myself sink down to another place, somewhere where Ben still sits beside me and massages my neck while we watch the TV.

The following morning brought fresh news via Jane, who had stayed overnight. Unusually, she was collected for work by her constable, Alf Tennyson. Shortly after dawn local celebrity portrait photographer Dick Izzard had been found unconscious in his small studio in Tankerton. Almost the last of the politically incorrect 70s shooters, his black and white pictures of actors and musicians of every gender wearing fishnets or strapped-up in leather had long fallen out of fashion. However, as a famous portrait snapper his work still appeared in local galleries and a retrospective distanced show sensitively titled 'A Feast of Legs, Tits and Bums' had been organised at Chattels before its conflagration. Alf had been to the scene early and was bringing Jane up to speed over her morning coffee. I made myself inconspicuous under the table as they caught up.

'He's conscious now and I had a chat with him before the ambulance arrived,' said Alf.

'Did he see who did it?'

'Two blokes in balaclavas. One was young and the other fat and middle-aged.'

'Same description as the two thugs who beat up old Jo Turnery down past Seasalter last week,' said Jane.

My ears pricked up and I edged closer to Alf's leg. Jo Turnery was Whitstable's most celebrated landscape artist. His fiery sunsets from Whelkville ranked high among the glories of Kentish civilisation. Alf let his left arm fall below the table and stroked my head as he spoke to Jane. Once more, I was hiding in plain sight.

'Yes, but there are differences that don't make sense, guv,' he said.

'How so?'

'Well, old Jo was told to not come round Seasalter again if he knew what was good for him. In fact, he was specifically told to stick to painting Whitstable sunsets, the Ancient Poseidon and the boats in the harbour. Odd, no?'

'Very – what about Dick Izzard?' said Jane.

'Well, he was just told to leave town and given a good kicking into the bargain,' said Alf.

'Poor sod – anything else?'

Alf took out his notebook and flicked it open.

'Well, they didn't touch his cameras or kit but they took all his pic props. High heels, thigh-length boots, tights of various meshes, cat-suits, studded belts, latex, spandex, leather, you name it. He says he's ruined.'

'The essential tools of his trade,' mused Jane.

Quite, I thought to myself. And it was pretty obvious where the Kincaids would strike next. I started to edge away from my cat-trained fuzz.

'How is Jo Turnery, by the way?' said Jane.

Alf sighed.

'Tough old bird, Jo. He's letting the world and its dog know he'll be back out in Seasalter with his easel and paintbox as soon as he's up and about. He also refused police protection.'

I stopped in my tracks. If Jo was ignoring the threat he was in deadly danger. The Kincaids didn't give multiple warnings. I'd have to step on it.

I found Ross was lying on his back in his donut, eyes closed, lost to the world. Lazy bastard – did I have to do all the thinking? I snaked out my right paw and slapped him on the kisser. He jumped up as if I'd plugged his nose and whiskers into the mains.

'What the f***?' he gasped, shaking his head.

'You, Lucifurr, me – Cape Cataveral, fifteen minutes. Get him there or else.'

I left him staring after me in shock as I headed for the Crab & Winkle. Sometimes you just have to shake everybody up to get a result.

Twelve minutes later Ross and Lucifurr crept into Cape Cataveral clearing and sat nervously in front of me.

'What,' I began, 'is the central concept of Situationist theory?'

Ross and Lucifurr looked at one another, then back at me.

'I thought you didn't believe in Situationism,' said Lucifurr.

'Yes – I mean, is this really relevant to the case...' Ross began.

I interrupted him with a savage hiss that made him recoil.

'I repeat, *what* theoretical construct is key to understanding the nature of present-day post-capitalism?'

Ross looked lost. Lucifurr slowly raised his right paw.

'Yes?' I said.

'The Spectacle?' he ventured quietly.

'VOILA!' I said. 'Lucifurr gets a fish biscuit treat. Ross gets to sleep in a dirty litter tray.'

I stared at Ross fiercely before continuing. He really was just a pretty intellectual lightweight deep down. Not so deep either.

'We see this phenomenon everywhere – commodities ruling humans who are reduced to passive consumers of the reified spectacle,' I said.

'What reified spectacle?' said Ross.

'The spectacle of Whelkville – mediated through fetishised images which have now become commodified,' I answered.

'Bloody hell, you've lost me,' said Lucifurr.

'I'm not surprised. You're a cat – you live directly. Humans live more and more by proxy. Their images are a substitute for the poverty of their daily existence.'

Ross started to nod his head – I could see the cogs slowly turning between his well-groomed ears.

'You mean all the pictures of sunsets over the whelk beds, dusk over the Ancient Poseidon, the red and blue fishing boats bobbing picturesquely in the harbour...' he started.

'Quite – those are the unrealistic sterilised images fed to the masses that descend on the town, to have the artificially-desired *Whitstable experience.*'

'Which means...'

'As far as the Kincaids are concerned, no other images can be permitted. This is what the great Debord calls the concentrated spectacle, based on violence, as opposed to the normal diffuse spectacle based on seduction.'

'My God – you can't mean the attacks on old Jo Turnery and Dick Izzard are *theoretically-based*?' gasped Ross.

'Of course. Jo Turnery's latest creative outpouring is in the wrong place, Seasalter. Dick Izzard's images of local folk posing uncomfortably in leatherette and PVC outfits are both too passé and too aesthetically subversive,' I replied.

'But how does the kidnapping of Dongal McDill fit into this?' Lucifurr asked.

'By providing an ironic self-aware commodity alternative for the more woke elements that turn up here from London at weekends. By appropriating his crude sexual innuendo images and incorporating them into a liberal mainstream narrative. Hence the stereotyped Whittywoke man character they have forced McDill to draw.'

'Concentrated violence? Bloody hell, I'm all for violence if there's a meal at the end of it. But not to undermine artistic endeavour. So, what praxis can we apply to resolve this?' asked Lucifurr.

'Yes, difficult to explain this deconstruction to the local plods,' said Ross.

'We must follow the dialectical logic of their analysis. There is only one local artist left who the Kincaid *père et fils* need to take out if they are to assert complete dominance over the spectacle of Whitstable. We have to stop them.'

I watched realisation dawn upon them slowly.

'No way can they touch him!' they miaowed in unison.

'You're right,' I said, 'we can't let it happen.'

Two nights later we were hidden in the Oxford Street alleyway opposite Chattels watching for any movement in and around the dimly lit shops. The church clock had just rung twice and now the heavy silence of the darkness had reasserted itself. A dark XJS with blacked-out windows had cruised by fifteen minutes earlier but otherwise the street was deserted.

At last we heard the approach of chunky bicycle wheels. A slim figure wearing a hoodie and a lower face-covering slid his BMX bike to a stop outside the burnt-out facade of Chattels. He looked around as he removed a rucksack from his shoulders and laid it against the plain whitewashed sidewall of the gallery. We peered out from the alley as he removed stencils and spray paint from the bag and arranged them on the pavement.

'Moggsy,' whispered Ross reverentially.

Things happened quickly after that. As if from nowhere the XJS roared up to the pavement and two men with balaclavas and baseball bats stepped out. I felt my fur puff up in horror. One of the men swung the baseball bat at Moggsy, who ducked and kicked his assailant between the legs. As the attacker screamed and fell there was a piercing whistle and

106

shouting. Jane and half a dozen uniformed coppers exited the burnt-out gallery and converged on the scrap. They quickly overpowered the attackers and removed their balaclavas to reveal Pop and Billy Kincaid.

Jane approached Moggsy and spoke to him. I prayed she would not ask him to reveal himself, but he removed his face bandana and lowered his hood even as I thought it. To reveal the smiling face of Alf Tennyson.

I was so shocked that it was only later that I remembered the low female chuckle behind us in the darkened alley. But the commotion had resulted in lights coming on in the houses and flats around Chattels gallery. We slipped away like ghosts into the darkness.

It was another Sunday lunchtime in Grace's house. Jane was cooking her signature pumpkin and spinach dal while she explained the case. Grace had just pulled the cork out of a bottle of their favourite Chablis. They took a moment to fill their glasses and toast each other. I hung around my bowl, pretending to be a greedy sod. I'm getting good at this hiding in plain sight stuff.

'Alf spotted some stories on the Whitstable arty sites that Moggsy was due to comment on the local art scene. That's code for another piece of graffiti on the High Street,' said Jane.

'What was Alf doing on those sites?'

'Using his initiative – creatives can't keep their traps shut,' said Jane.

Especially if they are using false Facebook and Twitter accounts, I thought to myself. Humans are so easy.

'We were already following an anonymous tip-off on the recent anti-artist assaults and keeping tabs on the Kincaids. We discovered they were cruising Whitstable late at night – obviously looking for Moggsy at work. They were also visiting the house in Seasalter where they were keeping Dongal McDill.'

'So you dreamt up the false Moggsy sting,' said Grace.

'We couldn't wait for him to show up and get hurt,' said Jane, downing the glass in one. Classy lady. So easy to manipulate, too.

'But why attack Moggsy, or Izzard or Turnery? Or lock up poor old McDill?'

'When we raided the Seasalter place, Krayfish House, we also found Pop's notebook. He had a portfolio of artists, some who didn't fit, like Izzard, crossed out, and others with ticks against the names, like Turnery and McDill.'

'Well, the bastards have been locked up at last – thank God.'

'Yep, kidnapping, assault, possibly arson and fraud if we can make them stick.'

I smiled inwardly at this atheoretical discourse. Yes, I was pleased at the outcome of the case. Grace was safe, and a measure of retribution had been achieved, though the big prize of head honcha 'Wild Hog' Fenella would have to wait awhile. But Jane had only succeeded in re-establishing the old art order. Now we would return to the diffuse spectacle, with hundreds or thousands of competing images of commodities preventing humans in Whelkville from experiencing the whole rich reality of existence as we cats can. I could not help feeling sorry for these two alienated and exploited bipeds as I headed into the garden. Time for a rest in Cape Cataveral, I thought.

It was dark when I awoke to find Ross and Lucifurr sitting next to me in the clearing. Their eyes were shining in the moonlight.

'Everything OK?' I said, sitting up.

'You gotta see this,' said Ross.

'What?'

'Follow us,' said Lucifurr.

We descended the hill into town via the back alleys, skipping into manicured gardens at the approach of stray dog walkers and crossing the quiet Sunday streets only when necessary. Finally we reached the viewing spot opposite Chattels. To my surprise, Ross and Lucifurr stepped out of the shadows onto the pavement.

'Hang on,' I said, 'what are you doing?'

That's when I saw it. The biggest, baddest stencil graffiti I'd ever seen, covering most of Chattels' side wall. And the colours were garish and loud, the style of the figures unmistakable. The McDill aesthetic on the Moggsy form – genius. Too big to nick and to sell. And the subject! Three enormous cat figures marching towards the viewer against a backdrop of mean Whitstable streets, one black, one tabby, and in the centre, their speckled ginger leader. And above the town, in enormous letters the motto 'THE CAT AVANT-GARDE WILL NEVER GIVE UP!'.

'Well, she knows her art history,' I said at last.

'She?' said Ross.

'She,' I answered.

6

The Mysterious Affair Of Criminal

Literary Styles

AFTER THE POSTCARD FETISHISATION CASE I DECIDED TO take a rest from the local crime scene for a week or two while I recharged my sleuthing batteries. Whelkville might be a fetid crime sink below its respectable surface but Detective Inspector Jane Austenson and her constable sidekick Alf Tennyson would have to cope without me for a bit. I knew that burlesque artist and DJ 'Wild Hog' Fenella Kincaid, the head of the clan, would be planning some rabid revenge on the town following the arrest of her husband and son. Between her beat-matching and nipple-tassel spinning, something illegal and deeply unpleasant would be cooked up and I wanted to be rested and ready for it.

But of course cat-fate had other ideas.

Apart from my sixteen hours a day of lying around, I instituted a rigorous fitness regime. After an early breakfast, achieved by scratching Grace's bedroom door to ribbons for about 20 minutes until she fed me, I'd saunter down the Crab

& Winkle Way towards town and sit hidden at the edge of the trees watching all the human suckers heading to work or school. They would pass a few feet from me, walking into a lamp post whilst texting, stepping into something smelly as they hummed tunelessly to whatever was on their ear pods or perhaps just rushing back to their houses having forgotten their face mask for the hundredth time. With humans, there is always something to observe and be amused by. They are dim but strangely fascinating and I'd always head home suitably thankful for my felinity.

Nevertheless, after a week of this low-level entertainment, I felt myself pining for stronger fare. And the next morning it slapped me in the face like frozen fish fillet. I'd just settled into cover overlooking the houses on the wooded side of Saints Road when I heard a low groan from the seldom-used unpaved alley that forks off towards the station between two of the houses. This was followed by a series of dull blows and more groaning. I edged through the undergrowth and looked into the alley to spy on the source of the commotion. A young man was kneeling on the path clutching his bleeding face while a masked assailant in flowing dark clothes and a hoodie stood beside him, holding a steel bar in a gloved hand. The young man had already been violently sick onto a pale T-shirt. The attacker aimed a kick at the young man's midriff that toppled him forward onto the path.

The victim's collapse was followed by more gut-wrenching violence rained on him from above. I'd seen enough. I raced back up the alley until it opened into Saints Road and looked around. But the street was empty, since those commuting had already left for work and the kids had not yet passed on their way to school.

Then I saw a young woman in running gear jogging up the road before slowing to enter one of the small front gardens. She looked at her plants for a few seconds and walked towards the front door. In another moment she'd disappear inside. I tensed myself and let out the loudest yowl I could before toppling over on the pavement as if I'd been shot.

She looked around and spotted me immediately. I let out a couple more pitiful miaows.

'Oh, you poor little thing,' she said, running towards me. As planned, just as she reached me she noticed the attack in the alley behind me.

'Stop that,' she shouted out.

She reached for her phone as I sat up and slipped away.

Works every time.

Twenty minutes later, I watched from the undergrowth as the paramedics lifted the stretcher and carried the young man into the ambulance. The doctor in attendance packed up her gear as she spoke to Alf Tennyson, Jane Austenson's deputy.

'We think he has had a fit caused by the blows to the head. He's in bad shape but thanks to this young lady we just got to him in time,' she said.

Alf smiled at the jogger. Indeed, he looked as if he was having a hard time looking at anything else at the scene, let alone maintaining his social distancing.

'And your name, Miss?'

'Ms Andrea Dutch. I work in publishing – but from home at the moment, obvs. I looked through his wallet – I thought he might be having an epileptic fit,' she said.

She handed the threadbare wallet to Alf along with the discarded parka jacket she'd picked up off the path.

'I couldn't find a phone – I guess the attacker took it.'

'Thanks,' said Alf, 'we'll get these to the victim in hospital.'

He gave her his best crooked smile and looked through the wallet quickly. I could see him counting a few notes and putting them back. He moved on to inspect the cards.

'Here we are, driving licence. Mr Che Koff, address 23 Downs Street. And a lecturer ID card from the University's Computer Studies Department. So he's local,' he said.

The name had turned on a light in my brain but I couldn't place it.

Alf moved on to the parka and felt it carefully. He hesitated for a moment then turned the jacket inside out and pulled a thin, dog-eared A5 notebook out of a breast pocket. He leafed through the pages quickly.

'Anything useful?' said Andrea.

'Looks like poems, notes for stories and such like but no, nothing useful.'

She looked suitably disappointed with his sensitive response. Good luck with that one, Alf. But I knew now where I'd heard the name before.

'Last question, Miss Dutch,' said Alf, 'how did you come upon the scene?'

'I didn't really, I was helping an injured cat. Then I saw this man lying on the ground with someone burly attacking him. I shouted out and the attacker ran off towards the station.'

Alf sighed and looked around. I shrank back into the shadows of the trees.

'Gingery cat with black and white patches, was it, Miss?' he said wearily.

Later that evening I crept into the study and curled up in the armchair behind Grace's desk to listen to her taking part in the fortnightly online meeting of the WHAT Writers. She had been a member of the Whitstable, Herne and Tankerton writers for years, offering up her gentle romantic fiction for regular ritual disembowelling by the leading lights of the group. It was a rather sad addiction.

I watched the other four members of the short story group pop up one by one on the screen. First, as always, was the pampered middle-aged face and Joan of Arc pageboy cut of Marie Citron, historical novelist, who acted as the chair of WHAT. She had last been critically acclaimed so long ago that the book in question, a Roman Empire epic, had possibly been classed as contemporary fiction on publication. But the *grand dame* of the local writing scene never let you forget her top-dog status. Then came the sharp-featured and goatee-bearded Carlo Castanets, grumpy fifty-something purveyor of self-published spiritual sagas in exotic lands. Best known for a minor hit with the novel *The Teachings of Al's Chemist,* he often claimed to have cavorted with New Guinea cannibals and had peyote visions with Native Americans in the Mexican desert. He recounted these dubious druggie-dog tales whilst downing red wine throughout the online meetings, his contributions becoming ever more disjointed and spiteful as his wordy feedback dragged on.

Next on view was the fragrant supposedly thirty-something but only in her dreams Marge Alleyn. She hove into view crassly overdressed as usual, with the pastel interiors behind her somewhat at odds with her formulaic and very violent procedurals set in crime-ridden seaside resorts. Commercially, she was by far the most successful author in WHAT, with excellent sales of her latest offering, *Yet another Bloody Murder on the Pier*. And finally, late as usual, the youthful green-haired Raimunda Cava, who served up terse dark short stories involving angsty DFLs just about coping with the deprivation of insufficient vegan bistros within easy cycling distance of Whitstable town centre. These tales were naturally regularly short-listed in various national competitions.

Tonight, Grace was spared the usual humiliation of her efforts, as the conversation was all about the brutal attack on Che Koff, which had already made the local news. Che had been the sole poet and flash fiction writer in the group, but his short stories poking gentle fun at the locals had made him a bit of an outcast for some in WHAT in recent months, subject to savage disdain by the established writers. Castanets in particular had led a campaign to have flash fiction excluded from discussion in the group. That resolution had been passed, with only Grace and Che Koff voting against, a couple of months earlier.

Marie Citron had rung the hospital and gave the group the grim news.

'Apparently, he's still in an induced coma. It's so awful,' she said.

Carlo Castanets was typically dismissive.

'Hopefully no worse than some of the drug-induced trances a Navajo shaman once put me through. I'm sure he'll come out of it,' he intoned.

He's started early this evening, I thought, noting the half-empty bottle of Merlot beside Castanets's elbow.

'I can't help thinking that perhaps it might not have happened if we'd not been so awful and allowed him to continue contributing to the group,' said Raimunda Cava.

'No need to feel guilty, Raimunda darling,' said Carlo, 'none of us can escape our appointment with Samarrah.'

'Don't call me darling, you sexist sod. And don't quote bloody Maughan at me either. He's such an awful reactionary. But you're right on one thing — it's only *you* who should feel guilty.'

Castanets took another large gulp from his wine glass and smiled as he set it down.

'Come, come, you're understandably overwrought, but let's be fair. We all voted and it was agreed that such short pieces of 'flash' fiction were unfair on the other writers here. As Hemingway said, we all bleed just staring at the blank sheet of paper. For real artists it's not easy to push out our minimum of 3000 words every month. Che was barely writing 500 and yet getting all the benefit of our sensitivity and experience in his feedback. Put bluntly, he was leeching off us.'

'That's unfair, what about his poems?' said Grace.

Marge Alleyn laughed.

'But his poems were terrible!' she said.

'Yes, a couple of obscure non-rhyming stanzas attacking some poor local businessman for passing off frozen Cornish fish as local catch is not exactly Keats,' scoffed Castanets.

'For God's sake, Carlo,' said Citron, 'I may agree with you that he was more *agit prop* than real writer and that he deserved to go, but the man *is* in a coma.'

Carlo Castanets refilled his glass.

'Based on his writing, probably some sordid drug deal gone wrong, but I'll say no more,' he said.

'Well, I for one will be honouring his memory in my next novel by including this horrible attack in the plot. I can feel his muse pressing mine on to do it,' said Alleyn.

'You're all heart,' said Cava, 'but he's not dead yet.'

'Well, we all know why *you* are feeling guilty, Raimunda. Your short-lived dalliance didn't go unnoticed. So what are you going to do, Ms self-righteous?' snapped Alleyn.

'I will include a character in my next story who is searching in the psychic darkness for his true identity, perhaps for his real gender, and his oppressive or oppressed history. I see him as someone who came to a crossroads where he met his father figure in a savage reversion of the Oedipus tale.'

Following a stunned silence, Citron picked up the reins of the meeting.

'Right, perhaps we should move on...'

'Yes, I think I've just got time to knock it together before the Canterbury Short Story competition deadline,' interrupted Cava.

But Citron persisted in changing tack.

'I was thinking, that in the light of this terrible attack, we could clarify the rules for submission. We wouldn't want the authorities thinking we'd been a little, well, harsh on poor Che. So, rather than saying one has to submit at least 3,000 words, we could finesse it a bit.'

'What do you suggest?' said Castanets.

'Well, I think what we always meant was that the 3000 word minimum was *flexible*. So, one could either submit once you had 3000 words, say every couple of months. Or you could have some credit and debit as well, so that if you were a little over one month you could submit under 3000 the next or vice-versa.'

'Yes, that's definitely what I thought we meant,' said Cava.

'It's bollocks,' said Castanets, 'but we should certainly cover our arses. And of course I did also suggest the creation of a separate sub-500 word writing group.'

'Oh dear, I really can't recall, but happy to go along with your suggestions, Marie,' said Alleyn.

'Good, I'll take that as proposed, seconded and carried then, should there be any questions from the local constabulary. They want to speak to me tomorrow,' said Citron.

'Apparently he was writing something longer than 500 words,' said Grace.

'Really? How do you know that?' riposted Citron sharply.

'Oh, I bumped into him in the Fudge Box mini market down by the station last week. He confessed that his work at the university, writing his short stories and this mystery longer piece were exhausting him.'

'Tosh. I doubt he had it in him to write anything substantial, or else it would be the shortest novel in history,' snorted Castanets.

'Well, I had no idea,' said Alleyn.

'Nor me,' said Cava.

'Wonder why he told you?' said Citron.

'Well, he told me it would be a big surprise and asked me to keep it just between us,' said Grace.

'Well, I suppose I'd better mention it tomorrow,' said Citron.

No need, I thought. Grace would relay all this direct to her live-in partner DI Jane Austenson. It was a good job that none of the WHAT Writers members knew about Grace's private life. Marie Citron would certainly not have tried to retrospectively reinterpret the group submission rules if she had known.

When Jane had come home earlier I'd overheard her on the phone to her colleagues. Given the seriousness of the assault the police had visited Che Koff's one-bed ground-floor flat and been let in by his landlady. There they'd discovered the flat had been turned over and Che's laptop was gone.

Marie Citron cleared her throat.

'OK – well, shall we start with the writing feedback? Marge's piece is first this week,'

I slipped off the armchair and headed to my basket in the spare room. The rest of the meeting would consist of interminable self-serving 'feedback', sandwiched between paper-thin wedges of supportive ambience. I hoped they'd go easy on Grace's admittedly lightweight prose, but I needed to cogitate on what I'd heard. It sounded suspiciously as if Che Koff hadn't wanted some of the WHAT Writers to know what literary cocktail he was cooking up. That meant my next step was clear.

The following morning I assembled the team in my office after Grace and Jane had left for work. Grace's ostensible study being in fact my office, of course. Lucifurr, the sleek Bengal muscle of the operation, lay on the windowsill licking his paws – no doubt the final traces of some poor vole – while Ross, our podgy tabby brain box, listened intently as I recounted the developments of the previous day.

'So do you think that Che Koff was attacked to stop him finishing whatever he was writing?' said Ross when I'd finished.

'Possibly. It may be they were after something that proved what he'd written was true.'

'How do you know the robber wasn't just after Koff's valuables?' said Lucifurr.

'Because the wallet was not stolen,' I said.

'Still, even if you are right, the attacker might have got what they wanted,' said Ross.

'Possibly, but missing the notebook and battering Che until Andrea scared them off suggests otherwise. I don't think Che had whatever the attacker wanted on his person.'

'So it's probably at his place,' said Lucifurr.

'Yes, we need to get in there and look around – luckily Alf unprofessionally let slip Che Koff's address.'

'We'd better get our skates on. I guess whoever worked him over will also think of that,' said Ross.

'Is it really likely any of those losers in WHAT Writers are behind this?' said Lucifurr.

'I have a feeling something isn't right in that nasty literary cabal,' I said.

Lucifurr and Ross nodded. They'd learnt from experience to trust my feline instincts.

'So we'll need to investigate Koff, Citron, Castanets, Alleyn and Cava,' I added, looking at Ross.

'I'll have something by close of today,' he answered, leaping onto the desk and tapping on the iPad screen. Grace unwisely kept it in sleep mode and the screen sprang to life. And he'd watched her key in her pass code long ago.

'We also need to recce Che Koff's place.'

'I'm on it, Flic,' said Lucifurr, heading for the cat flap.

'OK, we meet at Cape Cataveral at dusk,' I said.

Having tasked the team I went upstairs to my basket

to have my well-deserved midday kip – that's what management is all about.

The three of us reconvened in our woodland clearing bordering the Crab & Winkle Way, which we had renamed Cape Cataveral after the Limbless Catalytic Burglars case. Ross briefed us on what he'd discovered about the WHAT Writers.

'Well, Marie Citron was easy. She runs a creative writing consultancy online called 'Epic Stories', which advises potential authors on the usual things; dialogue, plotting, creating credible characters and so on. It seems to be barely profitable though from the deposited accounts. She herself hasn't done much writing-wise since the early naughties. She had three novels published after the international success of her Roman epic *Livia and Augustus* but they all bombed.'

'Personal life?' I asked.

'Widow. Lost her husband to a heart attack in '97.'

'What about Carlo Castanets?'

'Ex-advertising executive and copywriter who publishes his spiritual tosh online. He had a brief stint in the Marines in the 80s but spent most of his career in London and New York and retired early seven years ago. Divorced three times. Keeps himself fit by taking part in senior triathlons.'

'Hmm, so he's a possible for the assault. And Marge Alleyn?'

'Brief stint in advertising, then TV writing. She specialised in writing for adaptations of crime fiction. She worked on *Inspector Morose* and *Brine Suspect*. Then started writing her own procedurals about ten years ago. Her novel series about Detective Couscous of Herne Bay CID, the half-Mongolian, one-armed, alcoholic, sexually ambivalent capoeira champion and quirky pier performance artist, was a big hit at first, but sales tailed off after the fourth book. Reviewers started saying the character lacked depth.'

'Or any vestige of reality,' I said.

'What is she working on now?' said Lucifurr.

'Her new novel series is about a half-Brazilian, cocaine-guzzling, one-legged transvestite and Irish stick-fighting legend who is also a *cordon bleu* whizz with a wok. Detective Borabora of Margate CID.'

'I can see the stretch,' I said.

'Yes, a complete change of style,' said Lucifurr.

'And so we come to Cava,' I said.

'Yes, recent joiner of WHAT. She's a part-time creative writing lecturer who is also a freelance editor according to her website. One of her clients is listed as Marie Citron – but no details.'

Some itch was stirring at the back of my mind but I couldn't put my paw on it. There were connections between Citron and Cava, and possibly a link between Castanets and Alleyn, but none of it was enough to take me back to Koff.

'OK,' I said, 'we'll have to hope tonight's expedition gives us the answer.'

We jumped down into the small rear garden of the property in Downs Street shortly after midnight. Lucifurr had not managed to find a way into Che's flat on his earlier recce so we had limited hopes of success for this expedition. But I've always believed something will turn up and my faith was rewarded early. As we glanced around the garden shed we saw the lights were on in the two flats above Koff's. But that was not all.

'Look, there are some lights moving in his flat and the back door is open,' whispered Lucifurr.

'Bad luck. Let's head back then,' said Ross.

'Don't be even more of a pussy than you already are,' I said.

'I'm not going in there!' Ross said.

'Neither of you are, I'm going in alone,' I said.

'In your dreams,' said Lucifurr.

Without waiting for a response he skipped across the small garden towards the open rear door. I turned to Ross.

'Come on,' I hissed.

A few seconds later the three of us entered the narrow galley kitchen and moved silently towards the sounds coming from the front of the flat.

We stopped next to an ancient standalone cooker by the entrance to the front room. We could see four figures dressed in black with their hoodies up moving around in the darkness. They were using mini-flashlights to examine the books on a rickety standing bookshelf and loose papers lying on a cheap fold-up table that probably served as Che Koff's writing desk. Humans have rubbish night-time vision compared to us and they can't sense motion in the dark well either. We were pretty invisible unless they shone their torches directly at us.

'We've turned this place upside down. It's not here and I want to leave now.'

It was a voice I'd half-expected but Marge Alleyn's posh

accent was still a surprise.

'Keep looking. There was nothing in the laptop I nicked so he must put his findings in the file Raimunda saw,' said a hoarse male voice I immediately recognised as Carlo Castanets's.

One of the flashlight beams played around the desk. Che Koff's SLR camera lay on the table surface surrounded by lenses and filters.

'There must be something here,' said a female voice. I clocked Raimunda Cava's *faux* East End street vowels.

'He works in IT, so look for USB drives,' said another voice, deeper and plummier. So Marie Citron was also getting into breaking and entering.

'Stop, I thought I heard something,' said Alleyn.

'Nerves, dear, that's all. Let's just find what we are looking for,' replied Citron.

We watched the unholy foursome shuffling papers and lifting out and inspecting the books on the bookshelf. Quite quickly we began to register an increasing number of sighs and grunts of disappointment.

'Nothing! We can't bloody find anything,' said Cava.

'Are you sure you saw it?' said Citron.

'Yes, it was a thick envelope on the desk, but when I spotted it, Che tucked it quickly into the bookshelf.'

'Why the hell didn't you just nick it later?'

'It was just a one-night stand, Marie. It was over in twenty minutes and then he laughed his head off when I begged him to stop his little *exposé*. Then called me a cab so there was no time to slip the file into my bag.'

'Ahh, the romance of youth,' said Castanets. 'That unedifying description of your sex life doesn't say much for your charms, darling.'

'That's it, I'm leaving – I just want this all to be over,' said Cava.

'Really? Well, just remember it's not my fault he recognised your writing style in that essay he marked. It's you who will lose your lecturing job, darling,' said Citron.

'Come on, Marie,' said Castanets. 'You have as much to lose as the rest of us.'

'Yes, it's not a good look, the great Marie Citron revealed as operating a cash-in-hand essay mill factory on the side,' said Alleyn.

'Essay mills aren't illegal, so I'll be fine compared to the rest of you. I'm just here to help you all. So stop arguing and keep looking,' snapped Citron.

'We've looked everywhere. The file isn't here,' said Castanets.

'I wish we weren't doing this, coming here is creepy,' said Alleyn.

'Look on the bright side, he might well never wake up. And it's his own fault for being so nosy and finding out about your creative copy-catting and my invaluable assistance,' said Castanets.

'He also found out about your mystical bullshit,' snapped Alleyn.

'Stop, both of you. I suppose we could torch the place if we really think it is here,' said Citron.

'There are people living upstairs!' hissed Cava.

There was a long silence before Citron spoke again.

'I guess not, then. Carlo's right, we'll have to hope Che doesn't wake up. If he does we'll have to think of some other way of ensuring his silence. Slip something into his tea, perhaps.'

'Christ, I wish I'd never met you, you monster,' muttered Cava.

'Yes, but you do like the finer things and those pathetic short stories just don't pay for them, do they, sweetie,' said Citron.

'OK, let's go before someone hears us arguing,' said Castanets.

'Under the cooker, quick,' I whispered to Ross and Lucifurr.

We just managed to scurry under it in time, shrinking as far back as possible on the ancient greasy lino.

Flashlights were turned off and we watched the literary burglars' shoes move past our hiding place. We heard the kitchen door click as it was closed.

We emerged from under the cooker and listened to the footsteps fading down the side path of the house.

'Oh, shit,' said Lucifurr looking behind me.

I followed his eyes. He was looking at the round brass doorknob of the kitchen door. No lever handle for him to perch on and open. We were trapped inside Che Koff's flat.

'You try to find a way out – Ross and I will see what we can find,' I said.

I leapt on the table and looked over Che's sparse belongings.

'Think, Ross. Che is a clever guy. If he'd wanted to hide something he'd written or discovered he would probably have done so in plain sight,' I said.

'He seemed to have two interests – writing and photography – and he worked in IT,' said Ross.

He leant over to flip open the camera's memory card

compartment and we looked at the two cards inside. A large Compact Flash card and the small SD backup card. SDs can save anything. It was a long shot, but worth it.

At that point Lucifurr leapt on to the table alongside us.

'No bloody way out,' he said.

'Never mind that. Can you press the release button?' I said to him.

'Are cats smarter than humans?' he said, leaping onto the table.

He applied his powerful paw to the card release. We heard the click and saw the SD card pop outward a few millimetres. Lucifurr pulled it out with his teeth.

'OK, let's get out of here, so just drop it,' I said.

Lucifurr looked at me, the SD card between his teeth, and shook his head in disbelief.

'Come on, we've got work to do,' I said.

'What are you doing?' said Ross.

'Re-planting the evidence, of course. So that even idiots like Jane and Alf can't miss it,' I said.

Lucifurr deposited the SD card beside the camera.

'Brilliant,' he said, 'now we starve to death.'

'Not if you get that thing down with a bang,' Ross said.

'What thing?' I said.

We followed Ross's gaze up towards the top of the stand-alone bookshelf.

'Give me a lever long enough and a fulcrum and I can move the world,' I said quietly.

✦

It was the next fortnightly Zoom meeting for the WHAT group

and I was watching Castanets brutally pummelling Grace's latest short story. Citron, Alleyn and Cava were also present online. Ross and I were lying on the armchair behind Grace.

I reflected on our narrow escape from Che Koff's flat whilst I listened. Lucifurr had leapt to the very top of the bookshelf and then turned and pushed his hind legs hard against the wall. He'd then jumped feather-like onto the table, away from the falling bookshelf as it had toppled with an almighty crash on the thin floor carpet. We'd crept out from behind the back door when the landlady had rushed into the flat to investigate the hubbub and then waited on the fence at the end of the garden until Alf and Jane arrived. When they eventually reappeared in the doorway we'd spotted Alf holding the bagged evidence. We knew our work was done.

Now Carlo Castanets was finally coming to the end of his diatribe.

'So, to summarise, Grace, there just isn't enough going on between the characters. I know there's an extended, intimately intense conversation followed by the sex scene, after which the husband bursts into tears, but somehow it doesn't feel sufficiently emotional...'

His comments trailed off into silence as Grace moved and her form in the chair was replaced by DI Jane Austenson. She held up her ID and identified herself.

'Thanks to Grace for letting me speak to you all tonight. I'm investigating the serious assault on Mr Che Koff, ex-member of WHAT Writers.'

'Well,' huffed Citron, 'I really think you should have come through me as the chair. And I've already spoken to Constable Tennyson.'

'I really doubt whether we have anything useful to add to

your investigation,' chimed in Carlo Castanets.

'I'll be the judge of that, Sir,' said Jane.

She opened a file on the desk and held up the SD card we had planted on the desk, inside a clear plastic case.

'We recovered this disk next to Mr Koff's camera equipment a few days ago. It contains a number of documents.'

She looked at each of the four faces on Grace's computer screen.

'Ms Alleyn, the IT department of the University, where Mr Koff works, was kind enough to let us re-run a sophisticated plagiarism programme Mr Koff had developed on a chapter of the latest Inspector Borabora mystery. It was submitted to this group three months ago and the results were copied to this disk.'

Marge Alleyn became so still that you would have sworn the screen had frozen.

'Why on earth...' she stammered at last.

'The analysis confirmed that the chapter is heavily drawn from the works of half a dozen thriller and mystery writers. It seems to consist of cut up and mixed sections of others' work to create your fiction, if we can call it that. Hence the bizarre yet curiously derivative nature of your lead characters,' said Jane.

'Don't say anything else without a lawyer present,' said Castanets.

Jane ignored the interruption.

'I put it to you, Ms Alleyn, that you used this group to launder your plagiarism by incorporating the most inane comments of its members to further edit the text so that your deception would not be detected.'

'You can't prove any of this!' said Castanets.

'I assure you we can, Mr Castanets. Further inquiries at the Oxford Street Book Bazaar also revealed that you, Mr Castanets, have purchased hundreds of paperback crime novels over the last few years.'

'So I'm a big reader,' said Castanets.

'Yet it is curious that I can see that your bookshelf behind you contains no examples of the genre. In addition, an examination of your recycling bin yesterday revealed hundreds of loose pages torn from such paperbacks.'

I was enjoying watching the change of colour on Castanets's face.

'I like to do my bit for the environment,' he muttered.

'I put it to you, Ms Alleyn, that Mr Che Koff confronted you after carrying out his plagiarism analysis and you then told Mr Castanets, who was your accomplice.'

'I'm ruined, Carlo,' cried Alleyn.

'Shut your mouth, Marge,' snarled Carlo.

He addressed Jane directly.

'Officer, you need to understand that this is post-modern fiction, drawing on a variety of sources and styles...'

'OK, it's post-modern plagiarism,' said Jane, 'tell it to the publisher.'

'No, I can't bear it any more!' shouted Alleyn. 'I admit it, I offered Che money! A lot of money! But he laughed at me.'

She was now wiping her tears with the puffed-up sleeves of her house robe, smearing her dark eye make-up over her cheeks.

'Thank you, Ms Alleyn. Mr Castanets, analysis of your best-known work, *The Teachings of Al's Chemist,* using Mr Koff's software programme shows that it is in fact a translation of a previously anonymous and unpublished 1920s fantasy work written in impenetrable Georgian script.'

'Rubbish, prove it,' said Castanets.

'Thank you, I will. The recent rediscovery and translation by academics with not much to do otherwise has revealed it to be the only known novel by literary prankster Borgia Georges. A month ago it was placed on a worldwide database of spuriously spiritual literature and thus included in Mr Koff's programme search.'

Castanets suddenly looked as if he'd had the stuffing knocked out of him. So much for the philosophical resilience message of his supposed book.

'OK, he found out and said he'd expose me. I went round to his place and begged and cajoled him not to but he laughed at me too and then threw me out.'

'Carlo, please say you didn't attack him!' cried Alleyn.

'No, I didn't, I swear. I just waited outside out of sight and then burgled his laptop when he went out,' replied Castanets.

'Ms Cava,' said Jane, in a dizzying change of direction, 'when did Mr Koff threaten to expose you for getting paid to write creative writing student essays?'

Cava's eyes filled with tears.

'A week before the attack,' she sobbed.

'How did it work?'

'Well, initially I'd mark down the first draft of one of my students' stories to really discourage them. Then, they'd receive an anonymous email encouraging them to take advantage of our creative writing essay mill company's service. The student would have to provide the idea, characters and plot and I'd put it all together. They would then receive an excellent mark when they re-submitted. After a while they'd be hooked.'

'But you'd then publish very similar stories yourself.'

'Well, the student could hardly complain. But they couldn't be accused of plagiarism either.'

'Except Koff worked it out. Why did you do it?'

'He discovered it when he ran one of my stories for WHAT through his programme which also included my students' essays. I told him I only did it because I had no imagination, knowledge of people or plotting ability, but he had no sympathy at all.'

She proceeded to relay her unsuccessful attempted seduction of the young poet in far too much detail. Sounded like he'd had a good time, though.

'So all three of you were humiliated by Che Koff. You all had a motive to do him harm,' exclaimed Citron.

'As you did, madam,' replied Jane calmly.

'Me! You can't possibly implicate me in this appalling imbroglio,' said Citron. 'It's quite obvious who here had the means and motive to batter that poor young man. We all know Carlo is a nasty piece of work, whatever he claims.'

Before the others could protest Jane held up the SD disk again.

'On this disk we also found a few scanned pages of a novel entitled *The Chosen Figs* by a writer called Mick Torn.'

'What of it?'

'When we ran the text on Mr Koff's programme we discovered it bears remarkable similarities in content and style to your own novel *Livia and Augustus*. I assume Koff confronted you with this?'

'It's an anagram. I can explain...' said Citron.

'Please do,' said Jane.

'I wrote an earlier version of the novel and had a few hundred copies printed by a vanity publisher.'

'What happened to the copies?'

'I destroyed them, I'm afraid, to prevent any confusion. And the local printing company I used closed when the owner died. Lovely old man, Sid was.'

Citron dabbed her eye unconvincingly.

'Yes, he was found at the printer's, slumped over his press. Convenient, especially as there is no ISBN number for the book either,' said Jane.

'What can you be suggesting?'

'Why use the anagram nom de plume?'

'Youthful fear of failure, of course.'

'But the K doesn't fit'

'Oh, my middle name is Katherine. Just a bit of poetic licence.'

'Of course, your own husband's name was Mark Citron,' said Jane.

'Why on earth bring him into this?'

'Because the term "mark" is often abbreviated as MK. Thus Mick Torn fits perfectly.'

'That's an outrageous slur on me and my dear departed life-partner!'

'And Empress Livia had a close partnership with Emperor Augustus too, that is until she poisoned him with figs smeared in aconite made from the monkshood flower. Was your husband aware of your own predilection in this direction?' said Jane.

'What nonsense!' exclaimed Citron.

'It's not nonsense that toxicology tests have revealed the presence of aconite in Mr Koff's system,' said Jane.

Citron leant into her screen with a smile on her face.

'I really must bring this very speculative whistling in the

wind to an end. And I can hear someone at the door. Saved by the bell, you might say. Goodbye, Inspector!'

Her screen suddenly blacked out, leaving the other writers speechless.

'What now?' said Grace's voice off-screen.

'She'll do a runner!' said Castanets.

'Don't log off – just wait a few minutes,' said Jane.

Sure enough, Citron's screen re-appeared. Except this time it was filled with Alf Tennyson's face. He was smiling and holding up a plastic evidence bag containing a small vial with a few drops of purply liquid. In the background, Citron could be seen protesting loudly while another constable put her in handcuffs.

'Hello, boss,' he said, 'you were right. The pathologist confirms that the garden is full of monkshood flowers. We found this in her shed.'

'Bloody hell,' said Grace off-screen, 'I'm the only real writer in this group!'

A week later Ross, Lucifurr and I were basking in the dying rays of the sun filtering through the trees around Cape Cataveral. I'd called us together as more details had recently become clear in the case.

'But what about this *The Chosen Figs* novel? Why didn't we find it?' said Lucifurr.

'Because Che Koff had lent it to Grace when they bumped into each other — though I think he planned it after being threatened. He trusted her as she was the only one who had voted against excluding him from the WHAT group.

Apparently he'd come across a copy in the Oxford Street Book Bazaar, quite by accident. Perhaps Sid the printer's copy when his house was cleared.'

'So Grace eventually remembered it?' said Lucifurr.

'I spotted it on her desk and worked out the anagram. After I'd read it, Ross and I dragged it into the lounge and managed to get it on the coffee table.'

'But Grace and Jane still didn't twig,' said Ross.

'No, they're not very bright. In the end, I had to start chewing the pages and ripping it up in front of them before Grace stopped me. That's when she mentioned to Jane where she'd got it from. She'd completely forgotten about it. You see, writers never return books to each other; or read them, for that matter.'

I had been placed outside after my deliberate bad behaviour, then watched through the sliding windows while Jane berated Grace after she'd explained where the book had come from. Afterwards, the detective had come to the window and stared down at me, slowly shaking her head from side to side, before letting me back in.

'Citron asked Koff to meet her at Coffee and Chronicles for breakfast very early on the morning he was attacked. He must have previously informed her about finding the hardback novel. There she slipped some aconite into his latte and followed him back through the alleys to his home, disguising herself with a dark face mask en route. When the poison started to take effect, he started to stumble around, but pressed on. When she judged the coast was clear she moved in with the intention of killing him with a metal bar, knowing he couldn't defend himself and that it would look like a blunt object assault. It was the fact he'd been sick that alerted me to poisoning.'

'And she hoped he'd also have the hardback of *The Chosen Figs* with him, which is why she wasn't interested in his notebook or wallet,' said Ross.

'So Citron encouraged Carlo Castanets to threaten Che Koff to dissuade him from revealing his and Marge Alleyn's plagiarism. She also encouraged Raimunda Cava to sleep with Koff to stop him revealing the essay mill operation and Cava's appalling lack of creativity. All to divert suspicion from Citron's much more serious crimes,' said Lucifurr.

'I know, she really covered all the bases. She'll go down as a Whitstable manipulator of legend. My guess is she poisoned both her husband and Sid the printer, when she realised *The Chosen Figs* was a work of genius. She changed the title and claimed authorship but couldn't of course repeat the trick. So for money she set up her dodgy essay mill operation, disguised as a writer's consultancy business.'

As I spoke I couldn't help feeling sorry for Grace. Che Koff had become a celebrity overnight, and his terrible poems had been picked up enthusiastically by Andrea Dutch's company. He'd soon eclipse the local literary scene. With the other WHAT writers now disgraced and scattered to the winds, she'd have to plough on without a support group and hope to be published eventually. Still, at some point you have to ditch the water wings and just do it.

7

The Conundrum Of The Choked
Up Tennis Star

THE FURORE WHICH ACCOMPANIED THE UNMASKING OF local celebrity author Marie Citron as the poisoning queen of Whitstable and the rest of the local literary scene as a corrupt cesspit of plagiarism cast somewhat of a pall over our little household. Grace sadly suffered a bout of writer's block, which deprived the world of progress on her saccharine romantic novel, thank Sekhmet.

But it was now summer and the re-opening of various businesses over the month of July gradually lifted the mood. Jane dragged Grace to the Tankerton Lawn Club for distanced social tennis to take her mind off her writerly constipation. Despite no more than average hand-eye co-ordination the pair was soon in the ladies' doubles team and playing or practising a couple of times a week. As luck would have it the public courts on which the TLC club played were accessible via an old overgrown sailor's alley that ran off the Crab & Winkle Way. The TLC boasts four courts, bisected by Annie Street, which joins the coastal road that runs behind the courts. Over the next few weeks I would occasionally pop down and watch of a Saturday, crossing the railway track and a couple of quiet streets. I would then hop onto a garden wall and up onto the roof of one of the garages beside the two west-facing side courts. There I was concealed from view by a camouflage of evergreen climbers on the ancient fencing. When I got bored watching Grace and Jane, I could always just bask up there for a pleasant hour and drop off into a long snooze, soothed by the soft sea air. Us feline girls love our little comforts.

You see, like most cats I love tennis. The only time of year I binge-watch TV is during Wimbledon fortnight. Only in tennis do humans display the degree of grace that approximates catdom. But it's more than the players. It's the pop of the ball off the strings, its rhythmic movement to and fro across the net and the rat-a-rat of a doubles net volley exchange that give me infinite pleasure. My front paw will unconsciously flick out towards the screen while Grace squeals with laughter behind me. But I digress.

The TLC's hard courts themselves have a pleasingly ragged feel, with their slightly uneven surfaces and spidery networks of cracks, each pair of courts flanked on the sea side by a tiny brick clubhouse which also needs a lick of paint or six. The western side one houses the club office while the one on the eastern side of the road holds TLC's equipment. The two courts on that side of Annie Street, though identical in their comfortable shabbiness, are usually reserved for 'best' – competitions and coaching.

Of course, the majority of club players are enthusiastically average but bizarrely imagine themselves to be blessed with the fluid grace and concentrated power of multi-Grand Slam winners. They consequently mishit balls all over the shop, including into the surrounding gardens and onto passing cars or pedestrians. To try to maintain their sad delusions of talent many soon succumb to the lure of Ray Gunn, the club's cheerful semi-pro who also runs the tiny sports shop on the High Street. He does a good trade heroically micro-adjusting pillow-soft looping serves and banana-shot sliced backhands for those who come to him for tennis redemption. But Ray switching on TLC's tennis-ball machine and aiming it in the direction of one of his more mature customers is probably the most entertaining part of the day. Children will appear spontaneously to witness some poor elderly sod being driven back onto the fencing, legs failing, lashing feebly at the barrage of balls like some demented musketeer. At the end the build-up of lactic acid reduces him or her to a slumping wreck raising a racket in abject surrender. At which point the assembled kids and passing dog-walkers give a little cheer and move on.

But unfortunately for the self-improver the ordeal is not yet over.

'And now for the backhand,' Ray will intone.

However, it is also a fact of nature that every small club like TLC also has one decent men's player. They were usually drilled from infancy by a parent who lived a sick vicarious dream through them. The representative of the species at TLC is the men's club captain Maurice Miner, who usually rolls in affecting his shaggy-haired chic look with his faded Indian Wells T-shirt, Ray-Bans and battered tennis shoes. His demeanour suggests the careless insouciance of a bleached beach bum and he seems to be catnip to some of the club's ladies. But if any male in the club has the temerity to edge ahead in a social match they'll either find their nether regions in the cross-hairs of Maurice's vicious forehand or that their every shot is now mysteriously being called long or wide. Maurice is in his late 30s going on eighteen and his despotic rule as men's club captain at TLC has been long and dishonourable.

So it was quite an honour, not to say pleasure, to witness his grisly demise.

I say witness, but the reality is I only saw the discovery of his passing. The Saturday morning in question was pleasantly warm and I'd been nodding off watching Grace and Jane play a doubles match against the local ladies' champions, fifty-something sisters Rosa Testa and Fi McLaren. Normally Grace and Jane would be getting hammered, of course. The champion pair were class and had been dominant on the local circuit forever. They were the glories of TLC, regularly dragging them up the local ladies' league. And Rosa and Fi were also respectively the chair and secretary of and fanatical fund-raisers for the club they loved. But today they seemed at sixes and sevens and had lost the first set easily.

On the adjoining court next to Annie Street three other ladies' team members played a more desultory game of Canadian doubles. Clearly someone hadn't turned up. Suddenly Maurice and his latest girlfriend Anka Sway, a recent arrival at TLC from airhead central, screeched up in his Land Rover. Anka leant out and shouted over, ignoring the fact that both sets of players were in the middle of their respective points. This caused Grace to completely miss a rare volley put-away and spit out an uncharacteristic expletive. All seven players on court stopped to stare in disbelief at the unabashed Anka.

'Hi there! So sorry I'm late this morning. Something big came up!' she smirked.

She flicked her thumb towards Maurice silhouetted in the passenger seat, his left arm casually slung out of the open window. As befitted his moody self-image he simply stared ahead out of his dark glasses.

'Come on, let's get going, Anka,' he growled roughly.

'He's so grumpy. Just need to drop him off in town, girls. I'll be right back!' Anka shouted.

The Land Rover jerked away from the kerb while the players looked on, then nodded in disbelief at each other. Jane mimicked putting her fingers down her throat and gagging. The quartet returned to their game, though Rosa and Fi's fortunes did not improve.

Maurice's Land Rover pulled up again about ten minutes later and Anka Sway finally joined her annoyed threesome with only about twenty-five minutes left of the session. Why bother? I thought. Not even enough time to play a full set.

Over on the coaching court I noticed Ray unlock the kit store door and enter, re-emerging a little later wheeling the dreaded tennis-ball machine in the direction of another quaking victim. Oh, goody, I thought. I settled down to watch the entertaining tennis-ball pummelling over in the far court for a few minutes until the heat got the better of me and I nodded off on the warm roof-top.

I must have slept for half an hour before I was rudely awakened by a piercing scream followed by shouts and cries from below. I sat up sharpish to look over to the source of the general commotion. Grace and the other ladies were gathered in front of the doorway of the kit store, Rosa and Fi consoling a distraught Anka in a semi-distanced way. Ray sat on the step of the doorway shaking his head, the tennis-ball machine beside him. His client stood beside him peering into the doorway. Then Jane emerged from the kit store a moment later and closed the door. She spoke briefly to the gathering before removing her phone from her bag and making a call.

I realised I only had a few minutes to examine the scene before the emergency services arrived. I hopped down from the garage and slunk quickly around the outside of the courts, using the wooden boards at the base of the fence for cover. When I reached the coastal side of the clubhouse, I sprinted across Annie Street to the back of the kit store and up onto its narrow windowsill. Behind the security bars in front of the tiny ventilation window, held ajar on the topside by a rusty metal chain, it was just possible to peer into the small storeroom through the grime.

Maurice Miner was not a pretty sight. He lay bare-chested across the entrance of the small room in his tennis shorts and shoes with a tennis ball in his mouth. Next to him was a battered tennis string winding machine and a string reel and a bunch of tools on a small table. A partly stringed racquet, presumably Maurice's, sat on the winding machine. But the string itself had also been used for other purposes. A length of it was wound tightly around Maurice's neck and tied to the door handle behind him. The position of the body, with knees bent, drew you to the conclusion he'd been kneeling on the floor facing away from the door before it had been opened. His face was swollen and the whites of his open eyes staring up at me had turned dull red. His hands were at his sides.

I looked around the rest of the rest of the room, which was filled with the usual tennis paraphernalia one might expect. Old spare court nets, a safe cupboard against the back wall, a large white plastic bucket marked 'recycling' containing spent and damaged tennis balls and some club signs and spare club racquets hanging on the walls. I realised we were supposed to think this was a sad case of erotic asphyxiation. Maurice Miner, flawed star of TLC tennis club, was being sold as a gasper.

Somehow I didn't buy it.

I awoke the following morning grumpy and exhausted. I'd spent the previous evening shadowing Jane around the house to overhear her side of various calls on the investigation of the case. She'd only let a couple of useful details drop though. Every time she looked around at me, I pretended to be cleaning my paws or looking out of the window of the study at the empty front drive. When she wasn't looking I stared at her intently to pick up every snippet of her body language. I even had the cheek to get on the sofa and sit on her lap while she talked to Grace about the case after dinner. This show of affection was a once in a lifetime event and didn't go unnoticed.

'Oh look, the little sweetie does like you after all!' said Grace.

'She's been behaving oddly all evening – almost like she's been tailing me.'

'Don't be ridiculous. Go on, you were talking about Anka.'

'Yes, it's odd that she was with Maurice. Not really his type at all.'

'Oh, come on, she was precisely his type. He had simple tastes – blonde and young,' said Grace.

'Except that she's neither a real blonde or that young. She's a prison officer based in Sheppey. She also owns a couple of properties in Faversham. Why would she join TLC?'

'That is odd,' said Grace, echoing my thoughts.

'She says she loves the town and spends a lot of her time here. Apparently met Maurice on a night out in the Fearsome Arms a couple of months ago and joined TLC shortly after.'

'What about Maurice?'

'Not an awful lot to tell. Grew up locally, junior county player, toured a bit in his twenties and dropped out of the game. I got the impression he fell out of love with tennis when he realised he wasn't quite good enough. Then he had a couple of convictions for wacky backy dealing in his late twenties. Things went a bit quiet then. He eventually got a job a couple of years ago in the county council's Planning Department. Kept that quiet though – he liked to give club members the impression he was a bit of a wheeler-dealer, not a paper-pusher.'

'Perhaps he was. Still a dealer, I mean.'

'Not to our knowledge,' said Jane, 'and it always comes out in due course.'

'So do you think it was erotic asphyxiation?'

'I think it will be difficult to prove otherwise – the simplest explanation is often the right one.'

'But how did Maurice return to the courts and get in the kit store without any of us noticing?'

'I guess we were focused on our once-in-a-blue-moon win over Rosa and Fi, as they were trying to avoid a rare loss. Ray had his back to the kit store and his client was fending off

80mph balls.'

'I feel sorry for Ray, finding Maurice like that,' said Grace.

'Oh, he's a tough old nut. Ex-para, Ray is, and he's seen it all. Anyway, I'm questioning him tomorrow morning and I'll check he's OK.'

I was just wondering whether I'd have to nose open the local paper on the coffee table and physically point at the property pages so that Grace saw the obvious connection between Anka Sway and Maurice Miner. But I needn't have worried.

'We are checking whether Anka Sway and Maurice were involved in some property development together. He had inside knowledge of any planning concerns with any applications she might have made,' said Jane.

It was hardly a motive for murder, but Jane was at least trying. I gave her hand a playful scratch by way of appreciation and leapt off her lap. It was time to brief Lucifurr and Ross at Cape Cataveral. Behind me I heard Grace telling Jane not to be such a baby.

I woke up about 2am with a start. Something was bothering me about the scene, but I couldn't put my finger on it. I slipped downstairs and out through the cat flap into the darkness. I didn't fancy crossing town on my own without protection so I hopped over to No. 2 and scratched on the cat flap. A dark shape appeared behind the flap and a moment later Lucifurr slipped out.

'So, couldn't keep away from me,' he said.

'Actually, I am longing for... intelligent conversation. But failing that I need a bruiser to watch my back while I check out the tennis courts for evidence,' I said.

'But I thought the rozzers reckoned it was what it seemed,' he answered.

'Maybe, but something is bothering me.'

We crossed the graveyard and slipped over the railway bridge into Tankerton. Most cats are crepuscular in their hunting habits, and our growing popularity does mean that we are ever more likely to bump into each other in the dark. Shrinking territories means more argy bargy in the competition for food. Especially the way we reduce the bird, small mammal and invertebrate population. But with Lucifurr alongside the tomcats whose territories we crossed would slink back into the darkness.

We crossed the last silent roads and reached the courts about twenty minutes later. We edged behind the kit store and I saw that the ventilation window was still ajar behind its vertical rusty bars. I managed to slink through them and leapt onto the cupboard below the window. Then I started looking around the scene. Lucifurr was too large to pass through the bars and watched me from above.

'What is that awful smell?' said Lucifurr.

There was indeed a sharp pungent odour that pervaded the little room despite the air circulating within. Jumping up onto the table I looked over the tools scattered on its surface. A retractable knife and a large open tube of heavy-duty rubber bonding glue lay among the screwdrivers and clamps of the tennis string winder. I spent some time reading the club notices pinned to the wall and looking at the half-strung racket and the reel of tennis string on the table. Glancing below it, I could see the recycling bucket holding the old and sliced up tennis balls. I jumped down and nosed through them until I found an open tennis ball sliced almost in half. Just what I was looking for. I bit into it and lifted it out of the bucket.

My ears perked up. Outside, the sound of an approaching car engine had invaded the silence of the night.

'Someone's driving up!' Lucifurr hissed.

I took a last look around the room and leapt up onto the cupboard and then across to the small triangular gap between the angled open frame of the latch window and the ancient chain supporting it. I jumped but didn't quite make it, my lower body slamming painfully into the frame while my claws slipped back on the glass. In another second I'd drop back down into the darkness.

I felt something close hard around the fur of my neck to hold me in place while my back legs scrambled for purchase. I pulled myself up and lay for a second in an undignified mass on the glass surface of the window, the sliced up tennis ball still in my mouth. Lucifurr released his jaws' hold on my neck and I was finally able to inhale.

'Really not a time to start playing with tennis balls,' he said.

Someone was unlocking the door to the kit store.

'Shut up, you idiot. Let's get out of here!' I said.

We leapt down onto the grass and looked up at the light that had come on in the store, then edged around the building so we could see Annie Street. A battered red Suzuki carry van with an open load area in the back was parked on the kerb next to the entry gate. After a few minutes, Ray Gunn emerged pushing the wheeled tennis ball machine across the courts and outside onto the pavement. He locked up the gate and lifted the machine onto the flat deck, looking around before climbing into the driver's seat.

'Right, I'll tail him, you find your own way back,' said Lucifurr.

'What, you can't...' I stuttered.

But he was off, racing towards the van as Gunn gunned the engine, then leaping over the side panels of the rear deck as it started to move away and disappearing from view. He lifted his head for a second and looked back as me just before the van turned right around the Tankerton roundabout and disappeared.

It was late morning by the time Lucifurr reappeared in Cape Cataveral. He had quite a story to tell to me and Ross.

He had managed to read most of the passing road signs on the journey. Gunn had headed west on the A299 before taking the A2 at Faversham until he reached Sittingbourne. There he'd headed north and crossed a bridge onto the Isle of Sheppey and taken a smaller road towards Leysdown. But sometime before then he'd taken a right and then parked at a small lay-by overlooking a gated field beyond which Lucifurr could see a collection of large buildings surrounded by two lines of security fencing. He'd scooted off the rear deck and hidden under the van when Gunn had opened his door.

Lucifurr had watched Gunn unload the tennis ball machine and open the gate to the field before cautiously following him into the darkness. Gunn used the light on his phone to illuminate the control panel and carefully set up the tennis ball machine before loading it with a dozen tennis balls. Then he rang someone and spoke for a few moments. He returned to the machine and checked the settings for a final time. Finally he kneeled beside it and pressed a button. There was a low pop and a tennis ball sailed at high speed over the fencing into the darkness, landing somewhere in the grounds beyond. Gunn made a small adjustment to the machine and continued firing the balls at short intervals until the dispenser was empty.

'He lit up a fag and checked his watch. After about five minutes he rang again and spoke for a few seconds. He said OK, great and finished the call. Then he turned around and spotted me lying in the grass.'

'Christ – what did you do?'

'I growled, scooted out of the gate and hid under the van. I heard him laugh. After a few minutes he came out with the tennis ball machine, loaded it onto the van and got in the cab. I just had enough time to get out from under the van and jump on before he drove off. He got back to Tankerton and dropped off the tennis ball machine around 4am.'

'Well, that was excellent cat tailing. You'll be pleased to know that Ross and I have been doing a little background on Ray Gunn,' I said.

'Yes. Mr Gunn is not all he seems, but you really have to dig. Turns out he was discharged under a cloud from the Paras and then worked for a world-beating British industry,' said Ross.

'Really?'

'Yes, he was a mercenary, last seen on social media a dozen years ago training former African child soldiers for work in Afghanistan. And guess what we found online from his time in the Forces?' said Ross.

'What?'

'He was in a mortar platoon. So he's really just keeping his hand in,' I said.

'But what about the sports shop and the tennis coaching?' said Lucifurr.

'Oh, the shop is probably a front to launder the profits of whatever he's up to. And even bad people love tennis, unfortunately. Look at some of the big-name players.'

'Yes, you're right,' he mused. 'Towack Tohardovic, Frickn Furiyus, Shouty Slapitova to name just a few. It looks like it almost helps to be an arsehole to become a tennis legend.'

'Well, not quite. You could also point at...' I started.

We all looked at each other, stumped.

'Well, there's Baffer Banal, of course,' said Ross at last.

'Yes, lovely guy,' I said, 'I knew there must be one. Anyway, back to business. Ray is clearly a wrong 'un so I've given the plods a little hint.'

'You mean that sliced tennis ball?' said Lucifurr.

'Yep,' I said.

I knew Jane was interviewing Ray Gunn early so I'd left the sliced-up tennis ball on the pathway to Ray's front door shortly after dawn. Jane and Alf Tennyson had arrived at about 8am. I'd watched from the bushes as Alf kneeled to look at the ball. After a chat with Jane, she had put on her plastic gloves and put it in an evidence bag before dropping it into her coat pocket. Then they'd knocked on the door, which had been opened by a bleary-eyed Gunn, and disappeared inside.

By the next day both Ray Gunn and Anka Sway were in custody and shopping each other. That evening I got a full description of the case from Jane as she and Grace ate their takeaway in front of Netflix.

'Anka says she got a call from Ray very early the morning we played. He said he'd found their confederate Maurice dead in the kit store where they kept the drugs in the safe cupboard. But she thinks Ray killed him.'

'But how were they supplying drugs?' said Grace.

'They put them inside tennis balls they sliced up and then glued up again. Ray then used his mortaring expertise to fire them over the fence into quiet areas of Her Majesty's Prison Overwhelmingly on the Isle of Sheppey. Anka picked them up and then supplied the prison dealers.'

'Credit to Alf for spotting the tennis ball,' said Jane.

'Yes, he remembered that dealers on the street sometimes keep drugs in a sliced tennis ball,' said Grace.

'But why did Maurice have to be killed?'

'We think he had a disagreement with Ray. Anka told us that Maurice had applied for the lease the council had recently tendered to run TLC. And of course with drug money he could outbid anyone else. He'd planned to turn it into a private members-only club. Ray was completely opposed and much preferred a low-profile sleepy local club as a front. And Maurice had a drug record.'

'So the two men argued and Maurice was killed,' said Grace.

'Ray and Anka couldn't let their drug racket be discovered so they tried to disguise the death by putting on an improvised show. He slipped away with Maurice's glasses and T-shirt and got Anka to pick him up and drive round to the court. In the shadowed passenger seat with the sun high we all thought it was Maurice in the Land Rover. People would think he had been dropped in town and then disappeared. The plan was that Gunn would dispose of the body in the sea later that night.'

'But it all went wrong,' said Jane.

'Only because Rosa had a broken string on her spare racquet and went over to the kit store to restring it. Otherwise we might never have known where Maurice had been killed.'

'Will Ray be able to get away with it?'

'Well, he had motive, means and opportunity. His DNA is all over Maurice's T-shirt. And his glasses, which he forgot to put back. We can tie him to the kit store at the approximate time of death. I think Overwhelmingly prison will be missing his supply for a very long time.'

It was a week later and the July weather was glorious. The sun was high and warmed my fur as I watched the tennis from the garage roof. Fi and Rosa were murdering Jane and Grace – normal service had been resumed.

I listened to the pop of the balls on the strings of the champions. It was that lovely sound that had first put me on Fi and Rosa's trail. It was the strings, you see. Only Fi and Rosa in the TLC use the traditional gut strings. They give you more power and 'feel' and because they are more elastic they also sound different.

They wouldn't sound any different to an unevolved creature like a human, of course. Because while everyone knows that cats can hear much higher pitches than humans, few realise we can also discriminate much better between different tones and pitches. That's one of the reasons we hate so much of the crude human music.

When I examined Maurice's half-strung racquet on the

stringing machine at the murder scene, I noticed that it was strung with multi-filament, something that is a step up from the normal nylon most club players use. That made sense for Maurice. What didn't make sense was the open reel of expensive gut string on the table. One of the details Jane had let drop when I'd stalked her the evening after the murder was that Maurice had been strangled with gut strings. And I knew from a wall sign at the murder scene that only the club secretary and chair as well as the club captains and Ray Gunn had keys to the kit store.

I was already suspicious when I'd first seen Maurice's body that there was no reason he would be only T-shirtless if he had died of auto-erotic asphyxiation. Why not take off all his clothes if he was into this type of fun?

As club chair and secretary, Rosa and Fi often opened up the club and practised early on Saturday mornings. But on this occasion they had a reason for going in extra early and opening the door of the kit store. One of Rosa's racquets needed restringing and doing it takes a while. If they'd found Maurice cutting and filling tennis balls with Class-A drugs that would be bad enough. If they already knew he was bidding to take over the club that could well have flipped them over the edge and given them the motive to kill him. They had the means and the opportunity. With a two-v-one advantage, a *crime passionnel* of love for TLC was quickly accomplished.

My guess is that they set up the scene to look like accidental erotic asphyxiation and left immediately. Ray Gunn found Maurice a bit later and rang Anka. In their panic they concocted their deception to give the impression that Maurice's disappearance was unrelated to the TLC. Ray Gunn took off Maurice's T-shirt by first untying the gut string from the door knob.

I can imagine the shock Rosa and Fi experienced when Maurice apparently rolled up sitting in Anka's passenger seat. They were already playing terribly due to post-murderous shock. After he was driven off, they were in an even worse state. It didn't help that the local police detective was on the other side of the net. But they had to know the truth, which is why Rosa rushed to the kit store the moment the match was over. No doubt they were relieved to find Maurice's body, though *sans* T-shirt.

I guessed that Ray had taken off the T-shirt shortly after death and tried to put it back when he returned to the store and took out the tennis-ball machine. But by then *rigor mortis* had set in. Try putting a T-shirt on someone with their arms stiff at their sides. To be fair to Jane, establishing time of death is not an exact science.

I watched the graceful sisters swoop together towards the net for another easy put-away.

They are really making Jane and Grace better players, which is one reason I haven't shopped them. The other one is that I'm a cat, applying a higher morality to a very inferior species. Rosa and Fi are good people who happen to be murderesses. Their weird human guilt feelings will result in even better works for the club and the community it serves. Ray and Anka belong in the slammer and feel no guilt for their drug trade. It's not that complicated – and there's no need for Ross and Lucifurr to know the truth.

Of course, it would have been different if the sisters' racquets had been strung with cat rather than beef intestines strings. I'd have shopped them in a minute. But I love a bit of beef, me. I'm a bloody carnivore after all.

8

The Anti-Whiggish Winkle Iron
Footbridge Cold Case

WE GOT OUR NEXT CASE A COUPLE OF WEEKS AFTER I'D wrapped up solving the murder of the tennis player Maurice Miner, albeit by brilliantly stitching up a couple of innocent but very nasty pieces of work. That August Sunday morning Grace returned from the Fudge Box newsagents in very high dudgeon. I watched at our glass front door as she approached up our drive waving the rolled-up newspapers in her right hand like a cocktail shaker. What on earth has got into her, I thought.

I had to jump aside sharpish as she swept the door open and stepped into the hall.

'Those bastards have really done it this time!' she screeched.

Jane popped her head round the kitchen door and looked down the hall.

'You alright, hon?'

'It's those f****** PAWs! They are opposing the closure of

the WIF. The bloody thing is dangerous!'

'Well, hopefully the Council will decide to take it down. Breakfast is nearly ready,' said Jane.

Her face disappeared. I watched Grace still fuming as she took off her coat and shoes. She flung the papers onto the lounge sofa and stomped into the kitchen.

I understood her anger. Ross had recently given a short Zoom talk to a few of the local feline residents on this issue as part of his 'Weird humans: A natural history of your local homo sapiens and how to survive their bizarre ways' lecture series.

The early-19th century Winkle Iron Footbridge, or the WIF as it had been known forever, had been built to connect one of the sailors' alleys running from their modest houses to the shoreline. Originally incorporated into one of the town's bakeries, it had arched over the old High Street where it bisected Cutthroat Alley.

It was unique in two ways. When first built, you had to enter the bakery by a side door from the alley to use it. You then ascended the WIF steps that projected through the front wall of that establishment into the covered walkway. Both the metal covering over the footbridge and original bakery had long gone but part of the decrepit pale brick frontage of the departed building still attached itself to the crossing's rusting ironwork like a filthy ruff collar. This was because the bakery had been burnt down at some point and the frontage of the replacement building, now Bob's Butchers, had receded significantly.

The second curiosity was the original rationale for the ugly monstrosity. It had supposedly been built by famous Kentish Victorian entrepreneur Sir Robert Stealwell to speed up the arrival of ship workers and sailors at his boatyards sprawling on either side of the Ancient Poseidon pub he owned. Legend had it that before it was built these workers would be waylaid by the attractions of the twenty or so beer houses on the High Street and turn up at work blind drunk. Stealwell built the WIF into the side of the bakery, which of course he also owned.

It was believed that Stealwell had also done this in an attempt to damage his rival, Sir Jack Verily-Mean, the owner of much of the High Street, including those very beer houses that had sprung up like weeds after the passing of the 1830 Beerhouse Act. This included Verily-Mean's flagship, the infamous clothing establishment 'The Auld Grot Shop', the haunt of some of the worst tat of the town.

According to legend, when construction began on the bridge, this provoked several nights of alcohol-fuelled rioting, supposedly incited by Verily-Mean, and was eventually only put down by locally stationed army dragoons. At the climax of the fighting, the soldiers set fire to The Auld Grot Shop and forced its regulars to stand in a line before its frontage, noses inches from the flames, until they were suitably toasted. Flossie's Fish and Chips now stands on the site of the long-forgotten Grot Shop and its present-day clients re-enact the scene every Saturday night in a sort of unconscious folk memory.

Following the decline of the local shipbuilding industry, the WIF had fallen into disrepair and should have been put out of its misery decades earlier. Whilst it was studiously avoided by the locals, several unsuspecting weekending DFLs had perished by falling through its rotten wooden floorboards and rusty joists into the path of advancing motorists.

However, the Preservation Alliance of Whitstable (PAW)

had bitterly resisted the WIF's closure, citing its historical significance as a symbol of law and order and lauding its touristic value to the town. As well as holding the dubiously proud record of having opposed every planning application ever made in Whitstable, the PAW together with the Whitstable Ambling Footpathers (WAF) also pointed out it that it was a right of way, which to their minds rendered further debate superfluous.

This was a crazy interpretation, but given their political influence the PAW and the WAF had always succeeded in saving the dangerous eyesore, oblivious to the mounting casualty count, which probably now exceeded that of the original riots. Faced with another attempt to stop the slaughter, they had once again taken up arms to protect the indefensible.

I jumped up on the sofa and read the article plastered on the front page of the *Whitstable Wave*. The President of the PAW, Lord Dogg-Wees, author of the widely ridiculed history of Empire *We're Better than Them over There*, was objecting to the proposed closure of the WIF and the installation of two new replacement pedestrian crossings in the strongest terms. But more ominously the chairperson of the PAW's Historical Study Section (HISS), Dr Ron Scroot, was also quoted.

The HISS are the local intellectual storm-troopers of reaction and Scroot had gone to town on the heritage argument. He was particularly outraged that Dr Edwarda Gibbon, the head of the Whitstable Collection and Archive, had recently pointed out certain inconsistencies in the received wisdom of the origins of the WIF. Dr Gibbon was already not the local flavour of the month with Scroot. Her recent magisterial opus *In it up to their necks: Kent's Eminent Slavers of the 18th*

158

century had made a lot of the local great and good feel rather uncomfortable in their fine houses. However, she seemed to have been cowed into silence after being loudly disparaged by Scroot in the local press.

I heard Grace and Jane approaching the lounge carrying their breakfast trays. There was only time to sprawl across the paper and pretend to be cleaning myself.

'She loves lying on paper, does little Flic,' said Grace as she sat down.

'Yes, and always when you've just bought the local one,' said Jane.

She eyed me suspiciously as she laid her tray on the coffee table and shooed me off the sofa.

'She's probably better informed about local news than we are,' she said.

'Actually, she does that with the nationals as well. And I often find Ross sleeping on the open pages of my bedtime book,' said Grace.

I made a mental note to have a word with Ross about that. Not that this couple of thickos would ever put two and two together. In olden times, everyone knew that cats were familiars for many wise women and could read and communicate with them. They helped them prepare socially useful concoctions and the odd poisoning mix very effectively. I looked up at Grace and Jane filling their faces with tasteless fat-free yoghurt mixed with birdseed or whatever they ate and realised that the loss of the ancient ways must be something to do with their diet. Now there was a project for Edwarda Gibbon to get her teeth into.

I went upstairs and sat on the windowsill, gazing out past the garden and over the trees edging the Crab & Winkle Way.

This was a crime but not one I could solve. It was peculiar to these primitive bipeds to accept a 'natural' rate of unnecessary deaths rather than do the obviously sensible thing. Take air quality, sugar in everything and climate change, to name just three examples. Eventually, either some egregious event suddenly woke them up or they just got bored of that particular death wish. It might be a long wait for either in this case – I suspected the WIF would still be rotting proudly on the High Street when we were all dust.

The following morning I awoke with a strange sense of foreboding. It was bright but cool for mid-August and I could feel the weather was turning thundery. Holiday makers had been descending on the town in droves, no doubt including some of those Brits who had fled France a few days earlier to avoid self-isolation following the Government's travel announcement.

At around dusk I grabbed Ross and got him to accompany me down into the town, using the old overgrown Cutthroat Alley to approach the High Street. I knew that by the time we got there most of the locals and visitors would have slipped home for their dinners. On the way there I explained to him why I wanted to look at the WIF. We eventually reached the High Street and peered around the corner of Bob's Butchers.

As ever my feline instinct and timing was spot-on. The two face-masked people examining the remains of the old wall encrusted on the iron work of the WIF were so engrossed in their work we could observe them at leisure. A young red-haired woman with large, rounded tortoiseshell glasses set on a narrow face was furiously excavating the powdery mortar with a metal fork-like tool. Behind her, a small ancient man leaning on a walking stick peered around into the cloud of dust she was producing. She carefully removed three of the ancient bricks and passed them back to her confederate who set them on the ground. Then she leant back and cleaned away the debris of the dig from her glasses.

'Do you see, Dr Gibbon? Do you see?' cried the old man.

She put her glasses back on and peered into the gap.

'I do, Professor Ulay. This will set the cat among the pigeons. But let's cover it up for now. The fish and chips crowd will be heading down to Flossie's soon,' she answered.

I've got a soft spot for red-heads so I let the pigeons slur pass. But cat among the fledglings is surely the right expression. Ross and I watched from the shadows as Edwarda Gibbon used her phone to take a number of pictures of whatever they'd uncovered. Then the two of them pushed the bricks back into the hole they had created and wedged them into place with the cracked pieces of mortar littered around their shoes. When they'd finished they faced each other and shook hands very formally.

'Congratulations, Dr Gibbon,' said the elderly gentleman.

'The credit is all yours. It is high time to restore the distinguished name of Mack Ulay to the first rank of our profession,' said Edwarda Gibbon, looking down at him.

'Most kind, dear, I'll see you at the council planning meeting next Wednesday. Now, I must get in Flossie's queue for my cod and chips. It's a tradition, after all.'

'We'll put things to rights, Professor,' she said.

He nodded, I thought a little sadly. She watched him totter off towards the town centre, her eyes unsmiling behind her outsized glasses.

I glanced at Ross.

'Let's do a detailed background check on any history between Professor Mack Ulay and the HISS,' I said.

'I'm on it,' he replied.

'I suppose we'll read all about this discovery in next week's planning report in the *Whitstable Wave*' I said.

When I look back now I suppose I should have foreseen at that moment that those who sought to control the past of the town would stop at nothing to control its future. And to do that they would need to silence the historians in the present. But I let the thought slip over me like a passing seagull and then it was gone. So, without further chit-chat, we turned back to return to our eyrie above the town's streets and let the darkness close around us.

It was 6am the next morning when Jane received the call from the station. She rose and took the call in the spare bedroom so as not to wake Grace. I sprinted up the stairs from the study and listened to her for a second from outside the room. Then I wandered in and sat in the doorway while she spoke in a hushed voice into the phone.

'Couldn't he simply have wandered off and forgotten where he lived, Alf? After all he is getting on a bit,' she said.

She listened to the reply.

'OK, put out an alert and get round to his place again. I'll join you in a bit.'

She put the phone down and headed back into the bedroom. I followed close behind.

'What's happened?' said Grace, sitting up in the darkness.

Jane was already stepping into her service trousers.

'Sorry, hon. Looks like a kidnapping. An old, retired history professor called Mack Ulay seems to have been forced into the boot of a car when he opened his front door around 2am. He's in his late 80s and not in the best of health.'

'Well, that is a strange one. Who called it in?'

'The next-door neighbour, who is a local potter. She was up late on her pottery wheel in her studio, which faces onto the street. She heard the hubbub and when she looked out of her window she saw a couple of people in balaclavas pushing him into the boot and driving off. No details of the vehicle apart from it being "big and dark".'

She had finished getting dressed and stood up. She leaned over and kissed Grace. She nodded towards me.

'Little Miss Nosy has been following me around. Best get up and feed her.'

'She can bloody well wait,' said Grace, burying herself back under her duvet.

After Jane had driven off, I returned to the study where Ross was wrapping up his night of research.

'Well?' I said, settling into the armchair by the window.

'Welcome back and thank you to you too,' he said, without looking round.

He deleted the search history with his claw and pressed down the iPad button. Then he flicked over the tablet's cover and turned around to face me.

'Professor Ulay is a disgraced man,' he said.

'How so?'

'Fifty years ago he suggested an alternative interpretation of Whitstable's history that did not find favour with the HISS.

His thesis was that most of the public amenities of the town were built as a result of popular organised protest. But it was all written out of history.'

'Public amenities? Such as?' I said. I was struggling to think of any.

'Well, mostly public toilets but including the WIF, for one.'

'But everyone thinks it was built by Sir Robert Stealwell as a philanthropic gift to the town to reduce drunkenness at work,' I said.

'Ulay's contention was that it was built by Stealwell but for nefarious reasons. The real story was lost in the mist of time, or rather suppressed.'

'That's quite a claim,' I said.

'It was explosive at the time. Ulay was then seen as a young whippersnapper disrupting the established order. He was challenged to prove his claims to a meeting of the HISS. The meeting took place in the packed upstairs rooms of the Duke of Cumbria, with the press in attendance. But on the day he claimed that the historical documentation he had assembled casting doubt on the accepted origins of the WIF had been deliberately lost by the head of the then recently established Whitstable Collection and Archive. The said head, a certain Ron Scroot, denied the accusation and Ulay's reputation was destroyed.'

'What an awful story.'

In my mind I saw the Professor's wizened figure bending forward over his cane. What had he uncovered?

Ross went on with the story.

'Ulay emigrated to Australia and rebuilt his career there. It seems he only returned to Whelkville last year.'

'No doubt to clear his name before it was too late,' I said.

'And it looks like someone wants to stop him,' rejoined Ross.

It was late in the evening before Jane returned. The whereabouts of Professor Ulay were still unknown, but Jane had made the connection with Edwarda Gibbon from correspondence found in his flat and she had been brought in for questioning. However, she had claimed to know nothing about Professor Ulay's activities in Whitstable or his present whereabouts. Jane was rightly convinced Gibbon was lying but had released her late afternoon and asked Alf to take her home.

I knew what had to be done. I assembled the team in Cape Cataveral immediately. Ross had already brought Lucifurr up to speed with developments so I ploughed straight in.

'I believe that Professor Mack Ulay was assisted by Dr Edwarda Gibbon in revealing the true history behind the Whitstable Iron Footbridge. But their researches must have got back to the HISS and they have kidnapped Ulay. My theory is that Edwarda Gibbon has been told to keep quiet about it, or else,"

'But unless they silence them both that only delays the inevitable,' said Ross.

'No. They only have to keep things quiet until after the council planning meeting next Wednesday. Once the decision has been made it can't be reversed except for planning reasons. Whoever really built it is not a material consideration,' I said.

'But they still have to make Gibbon believe that they will do harm to Ulay,' said Lucifurr.

Ross and I looked at each other. Local historians are known to be some of the most vicious human specimens on earth, up there with investment bankers and fly-tippers. But Lucifurr was an innocent on such matters.

'Ulay is old and frail. It wouldn't take much to tip him over,' I said.

'So where do we think they will hide him?' said Ross.

'If they are true to form I suspect somewhere in the area with historic significance, close by so they can keep an eye on him without being missed themselves,' I said.

'How do we find that?' said Lucifurr.

'We need to cover the bases. You will keep an eye on Dogg-Wees while Ross trails Scroot. They are bound to live nearby. I think we can safely ignore the Whitstable Ambling Footpathers – everyone else does. We're going to find out what Ulay and Gibbon discovered.'

Over the following days the team maintained a close watch on the three main actors in the Ulay saga that had unfolded. However, neither Dogg-Wees or Scroot made any suspicious move that would have led us to Professor Ulay. In fact, they barely made a move at all. Meanwhile, Dr Gibbon had also locked herself up in her home, having food delivered and rarely venturing even into her garden. We were completely stumped and the planning meeting was now only three days away. Police appeals for Professor Ulay's whereabouts had come up empty and Jane and Alf had no useful leads.

On Monday morning I reconvened the team at Cape Cataveral to review our options and brainstorm a way forward.

After an hour of furious ear-scratching it was Lucifurr who had the brainwave.

'What if he is being guarded by the Whitstable Ambling Footpathers?'

It seemed such a far-fetched notion that such an apparently inoffensive group as the WAFers should be involved in a kidnapping that I almost yowled in derision. However, something clicked in my brain. Was it really mad? Why were they not affiliated to the Ramblers? The paramilitary walking kit, the complete knowledge of every corner of Whelkville including hiding places in local woods and hamlets, the ability to spot others approaching with powerful binoculars and long-range camera lenses and to overwhelm them in large if geriatric numbers certainly made it possible that the WAF had abducted Ulay and were holding him somewhere close by. All psychologically camouflaged under a veneer of southern counties pleasantry whenever you passed them on their manoeuvres. They were invisible in plain sight, especially if they were distanced into small groups in a Covid-secure way.

Ross had clearly had the same thought.

'I checked the WAFers' Facebook page yesterday. It displays their planned rambles during lockdown. I was a bit surprised how many of them consisted of just rambling up Borstal Hill and over the roundabout to Wraik Hill.'

That was odd. Why walk up a hill beside a busy road then over an even busier roundabout for a supposedly healthy ramble?

'When is their next distanced ramble?' I asked.

'Today. They assemble in the car park of The Two Old Drunkards at the bottom of Borstal Hill at 1pm,' Ross replied.

'Well, there is no time to lose, then. Lucifurr and I will

follow the WAFers at a safe distance. Can you investigate the existence of historical sites within a half-mile radius of the top of Borstal Hill?'

Ross miaowed his assent and the three of us leapt over the garden fence. Ross pushed through our cat flap to start his researches. Lucifurr and I crossed the grounds of the Whitstable school to Bellevue Rd then slipped downhill through the allotments until we reached the houses lining the other side of Millstrood Road. From there we crept through the gardens of the houses until we arrived at the corner of Gorge Lane and the main road climbing Borstal Hill. A low wall arched around a commercial building on the left corner. We leapt over it and peered over at the frontage of the pub opposite.

There were already a dozen or so WAFers gathered in the car park. The heavy traffic whizzed by up and down Borstal Hill. They would be easy enough to follow – none of them looked particularly alert, but crossing the road seemed like a death sentence.

But we were in luck. An elderly rambling couple walked slowly past us and stood on the edge of the pavement directly opposite The Two Old Drunkards. They waved and pointed their walking sticks until some of the WAFers opposite noticed them and starting waving back. Their cries grew and filled the air and the two new arrivals suddenly jerked forward and started crossing the road at a snail's pace.

'Witowei! Witowei!' chanted the whole group like a bizarre black-magic mass.

The eerie sound was mixed with that of squealing brakes as cars and lorries brought themselves to a shuddering stop. A white van jack-knifed into the oncoming traffic lane yards in front of the female of the ancient pair. She turned to point her stick into the face of the driver.

'Tsou Witowei!' she screamed hoarsely.

The terrified driver instinctively crossed his arms in front of his face to ward off her curse.

'What the f*** are they singing?' I said.

'It's the ancient Kentish Right of Way chant,' said Lucifurr, 'They have just established a new spiritual Witowei ley line to the pub.'

'You are joking...' I started.

'It's to do with Kentish druids, but never mind all that. Let's get across – we'll never have a better chance,' he said, leaping over the wall.

Without thinking I scrambled over and followed him across the road between the becalmed traffic. By the time the couple had joined the rest of the WAFers we were observing them unseen from under a parked car. A few minutes later the troop set off up Borstal Hill in a distanced single file. We followed at a discreet distance, leaping over the side border fences of front gardens next to the road like Grand National runners.

About two-thirds of the way up Borstal Hill something interesting happened. The two WAFers at the rear peeled off and turned right down Meadow Walk. They were wearing broad-rimmed sunhats and neck gaiters pulled up over their noses, rendering them unidentifiable. I noted that both were carrying rucksacks that were rather overfilled for such a short walk. They glanced behind at regular intervals as they wound their way around the streets leading uphill. Eventually, they arrived outside a large house with a tall brick front garden wall. They walked up the gated entrance of the drive and glanced around before unlocking it and slipping in. We approached the gate just in time to hear it being relocked and the WAFers' footsteps moving away up the drive.

Lucifurr was already examining the brick wall for ways in. At the corner of the frontage I spotted a telegraph pole.

'Come on,' I said.

We scaled the pole and leapt onto the top of the wall overlooking the front garden. The house's doors and lower windows had been systematically boarded up, presumably to prevent burglary or squatting. The wide drive to the left of the building led into a very large, overgrown back garden surrounded by a thick border of mature trees. To the rear of the garden the trees formed a small copse, inside which a small low-rise building could be just discerned. We leapt down onto an ancient wooden composter just under the wall and then jumped onto the garden's thick, overgrown turf. At that moment, the two WAFers emerged from the copse holding up a hooded figure between them. They led him over to a rusty wrought-iron table and chairs in the centre of the garden and sat him down before taking their rucksacks off. We crawled through the long grass and lay flat only a few yards away.

The WAFers sat down either side of their captive and removed the hood to reveal a tired-looking but defiant Professor Ulay.

'Who on earth are you and why are you holding me?' he demanded loudly. He looked around the dense barrier of trees surrounding him and the back of the boarded-up house until his eyes alighted on the side driveway.

One of the WAFers lifted his rucksack onto the table and withdrew a thermos flask and clear plastic container.

'No one can hear or see you here, Professor, so just eat,' he said through his neck-gaiter.

'Yes, no funny business,' said the other in a high-pitched female voice, 'or you are right back in the slammer.'

'Yes, a curious construction,' said the old man, 'a World War II Nissen hut converted to a cell. Fascinating graffiti well worthy of a monograph on 1940s misogyny. You took the trouble to drive me around for half an hour in the boot of your car but I counted the left and right turns and the seconds in between very carefully. I believe I am still in Whitstable,' he said.

The WAFers glanced at each other.

The Professor smiled and bit into his sandwich, then made a face.

'Bloody corned beef on white bread delivered in a Tupperware container. You really do want to take us back to the past,' he said.

'You should never have come back, Professor,' said the male WAFer.

'Stirring things up like this,' added the female WAFer.

The Professor laughed.

'Indeed, I would venture that my accommodation is part of the old RAF Whitstable low level radar station on Borstal Hill. Long gone now of course to make way for the post-war housing, apart from the sprinkling of underground bunkers, pill-boxes and decaying Nissen huts in various gardens.'

'Very clever, Professor, it's a shame that you won't be able to display your expertise this Wednesday coming,' said the male WAFer.

'Oh, that hardly matters – truth will out,' replied the old man.

'I think he's hoping Dr Gibbon will come to the rescue,'

said the woman.

'Shut up,' the male WAFer said sharply.

Professor Ulay's head had jerked up at the mention of Gibbon. He looked at each of his captors then down at the ground, his shoulders slumping.

'Well, it's not the first time I've been shafted,' he said.

He stood unsteadily and spotted us lying in the grass. I could have sworn he gave us a small sad smile.

'I'm ready to go back inside,' he said quietly.

Ross was looking out of the glass doorway of our house as Lucifurr and I walked wearily up the drive. He stood on his hind legs, resting his front paws on the door, then disappeared. I heard the cat-flap click and a few moments later he was sprinting towards us.

'Let me guess,' I said, 'you have discovered that there was an RAF radar base on Borstal Hill during World War II.'

He looked a little crestfallen until we told him what we had discovered. His eyes lit up when we described how sad Ulay seemed when Gibbon was mentioned.

'Ah, yes, Dr Edwarda Gibbon. I found out something interesting about *her*,' he said.

'Spit it out, then,' I said.

'She is a descendant of Sir Robert Stealwell, who built the WIF. So it's surprising that she is trying to get it knocked down.'

'I don't think she is,' I said.

Lucifurr and Ross looked at each other. They were still behind the curve, but for me the disparate pieces of the jigsaw puzzle were falling into place.

I gave Ross a playful slap across the chops.

'Bloody hell,' he said, shaking his head.

'Good work, Rossy. Now we need to send out some more anonymous emails to the police or they'll never solve the kidnapping in time.'

Lucifurr lay down on his side on the warm grass and licked on his front paws. His work was done and he knew it. He looked across at Ross.

'Still here? You heard the lady – step to it,' he said.

I love work banter, I thought, as I followed Ross indoors.

It was the following Thursday evening and Jane and Grace were eating a takeaway in front of the TV. The local news had been full of the local council's preliminary decision to pull down the WIF following the discovery of a 'historic injustice of enormous proportions' as several local bandwagoning politicians had described it. This followed the anonymous tip-off and dramatic rescue of Professor Mack Ulay from his hidden Nissen hut two days earlier. Jane was giving us the inside line. Or rather she was giving Grace the inside line on my brilliance.

'We suppose the anonymous tip-offs came from disgruntled WAFers fed up with carrying out the reactionary wishes of the PAW and the HISS. At the end of the day all they really wanted to do was have a nice walk. Not stop all progress in the town or cover up historical wrongs,' she said.

From my armchair I glanced over at Ross lying on the rug by the TV. He winked back at me. We would never understand the naivety of this supposedly advanced species. It was true that many WAFers had left to join the Ramblers when the truth had come out, but a hard core of ambling druidic cultists were still out there. Still, it kept them off the streets.

'You said tip-offs plural,' said Grace, lifting her glass. Her favourite movement in the world.

'Yes, another tip-off led us back to Dr Gibbon, who was accused of being involved in the kidnapping in the email we received.'

It had been a nice touch by Ross to suggest sending a separate email incorporating Kentish druidic terms, as advised by Lucifurr. Our Bengal cat-hunk had often observed the WAFers' weird ceremonies in Blean Wood on his midnight hunts and picked up some choice phrases. So the note from someone who claimed not to be a nabbler but also didn't want to roil, and most importantly was not convinced that the WIF was a genuine weitowei, told them that Dr Gibbon was shuckish and the police shouldn't gollop all she said. They should search her house for clues on the motive, innit tho. It had taken the Kent Police Translation Unit specialists in Appledore a few hours to make sense of it.

Simultaneous raids had been carried out on the house on Borstal Hill and Edwarda Gibbon's home on Tuesday lunchtime. Once Professor Ulay had been rescued, Gibbon had cracked quickly under interrogation and the whole PAW/ HISS/WAF conspiracy had been mercilessly exposed. Dogg-Wees and Scroot had resigned in disgrace, their Whiggish historical nonsense discredited forever. But what was revealed from untangling their conspiracy of lies made the town gasp.

For the WIF had not been built to help ship workers to get to the boatyards by a Victorian philanthropist seeking to steer his workforce away from drink. It had been constructed by the forced labour of unemployed agricultural workers claiming poor relief, the same workers who had seen their wages steadily driven down by the likes of Stealwell and Verily-Mean. For these men were not only industrialists and shop-owners but also large local landowners. And the monument had been built to celebrate their tyranny.

'All of this had been buried in the bowels of the Whitstable Collection and Archive for two centuries. When Professor Ulay turned up after fifty years and started asking to see the records, Gibbon came across this concealed information. She then consulted Scroot, who told her the full story and forced her to go along with the deception and the kidnapping to protect the reputation of her antecedent. And his, of course,' said Jane.

'You mean the story of the Whitstabloo Charge,' said Grace, repeating the ridiculous name the local press had given to the newly discovered event.

'Exactly. The year before the WIF was built, a peaceful protest of agricultural labourers seeking higher poor relief and better wages and local people seeking electoral reform assembled outside Stealwell's and Verily-Mean's establishments in town. Unknown to them the authorities, encouraged by Stealwell, had called out the dragoons who rode down Borstal Hill and dispersed the demonstration with their sabres. This was the era of the "Captain Swing" protests and the upper classes saw any public gathering as potentially revolutionary.'

'But why don't we know about this?' said Jane.

I could tell that as a local, Jane was annoyed that she was unaware of part of her history.

'I guess it was over quickly with not much bloodshed, so history was quietly rewritten,' said Grace.

And everyone was focused on the new Canterbury and Whitstable railway, of course, I thought. Never mind all the starvation, hayrick burning, smashing up threshing machines, adult suffrage campaigning, judicial hangings and transportations going on, just look at this shiny new toy train over here. And was it a train anyway? The bloody fraud was pulled by ropes almost all the way to Canterbury! Human beings were just like magpies, drawn to shiny things.

'But the WIF was built to commemorate the putting down of the demonstration,' said Jane.

'Somehow, that triumphalism lost its lustre quickly, so all that was quietly forgotten. Ahh, the local news is coming on.'

Grace raised the volume with the remote. On the screen a journalist was standing at a safe distance from Professor Ulay under the WIF. In the background on the pavement, a couple of builders were carefully finishing the process of removing and stacking the top layer of bricks from around the uneven wall surrounding the entrance to the bridge. On the older brick wall behind it a message had emerged. The camera panned and focused on the large Victorian script.

'To Stealwell and Verily-Mean
Beneath your monument to tyranny
Sits our plea of poverty
All that we want is what we earn,
freedom by ballot or else you burn.
Swing.'

'So what is it, Professor?' said the journalist.

'It's typical 19th century graffiti, deeply etched into the brickwork, impossible to eradicate. Much more effective than modern acrylic paints in that respect.'

'So it was hidden behind another brick layer by Stealwell?' said the journalist.

'Exactly, though that didn't prevent his bakery being burnt down a month later, just like Verily-Mean's Auld Grot Shop. This graffiti is a priceless monument to the connection local people were making between poverty and political reform. By placing it next to the WIF it undercut the triumphalism of what was then and still is a reactionary monument.'

The journalist smiled and leaned in for the kill.

'So you think the WIF should definitely be pulled down?'

The Professor turned and smiled into the camera.

'It is for local people to decide of course, but perhaps it is enough that it is properly understood. After all, if we keep the graffiti, as we must, why not keep the thing it exposed?'

Ross fell heavily on his side on the rug and I miaowed involuntarily with frustration. Yes, dear reader, there will be years yet of prevarication on that old rust bucket.

9

The Star-Struck Allotment Scandi

Scandal

THE WEEKS FOLLOWING THE WINKLE IRON FOOTBRIDGE case were marked by feverish excitement in the town. A film crew had arrived to shoot the first novel in the famous Whitstable Whelk mystery series. Written by the world famous Scandi author Bo Leggido, they were notable for portraying Whelkville as the dark and unforgiving haunt of assorted psychopaths, reliving childhood traumas by lopping off the limbs and heads of local residents, usually until finally trapped and captured in some dank warehouse or basement by the hero, Cooki Cutterssen. Cooki, a hyper-intelligent-off-the-spectrum outsider disliked by everyone except her pet lizard, had become a cult heroine to readers looking for something grittier than the normal 'cozy' crime fare that normally depicted the town.

The buzz exploded into a volcanic eruption when Grace took a short call from Broderic Brassica, Chairman of the Seaview Hill Allotment Group (SHAG) on Saturday afternoon.

She shrieked with joy as she closed the call and rushed back into the garden where Jane was sitting sipping her post-work prosecco on the patio. Ross scooted off in fright, leaping onto the garden fence before turning to look back at his over-excited mistress. Jane looked up calmly at Grace from behind her dark reflective glasses and I didn't budge from my favourite spot on the cool thick grass shaded by the garden chalet. We hardened detectives are well used to Grace's little paroxysms.

'So?' said Jane.

'They want your allotment!' cried Grace.

'What?'

'The film crew. They want to film some of the first Cooki Cutterssen episode on your allotment!'

'Why mine?'

'Well, Broderic said they thought that compared to the others in SHAG, it's a bit shit, which is what the episode requires. Plus, it has a wonderful background view of the sea.'

It was Jane's turn to erupt.

'A bit SHIT?' she shouted.

Well, it is a bit shit, I thought. Jane had had the allotment for five years and done her best, but she had the reverse agricultural Midas touch. Everything she touched turned brown and died. Her wonky home-made raised beds, leaning tower water butt and wide selection of rare indestructible weeds were the source of much jollity among her surrounding lessees at the allotments.

All of which was made worse by the gradual encroachment of well-off DFL lessees on the site, with furniture-quality wooden raised beds in their architecturally designed and contractor-installed plots. In the one neighbouring Jane's, Ivor and Runa Bean either insidiously force-fed her their

179

intractably right-on no-dig philosophy in every 'casual' chat or loudly drilled it into their children, Bjorn and Friea.

So, on the days when the kids planted yet another row of perfect exotic carrot seedlings with all the joy of Russian gulag inmates, Jane was similarly miserable a few yards away, desperately trying to breathe life into an expiring lettuce. Or loading another bunch of Maris Pipers with the consistency of gelatine into her wheelbarrow to dispose of quietly at home. She'd gaze across at Ivor and Runa's oasis of verdant perfection and tell herself she was a tough-as-nails copper and so she would *not* burst into tears. She'd do it later in the privacy of her office.

So she was just a tad sensitive to criticism of her vegetable-growing skills.

Grace hurriedly apologised as she sat down beside her partner. After a moment of wary silence she spoke again, very softly.

'There is something else.'

'What?'

'They'll need to dig up your asparagus plot.'

'NO F****** WAY!' Jane roared.

'Oh come on, luv. Nothing is coming out of that bed you can eat.'

'You have to wait for asparagus,' Jane mumbled.

'Not five bloody years you don't,' Grace said.

Jane looked away. Behind her reflective lenses, was it possible that tears were forming?

'Why do they have to dig it up?'

'Ahh, well, if you'd read the first Cooki Cuttersen novel *A Crop of Murder* you'd know the answer to that. There's a corpse under a vegetable plot.'

'Well, I'll need to be compensated,' said Jane.

'They've offered a grand for a few days' shoot – SHAG will take half.'

Jane was silent – I could see she was considering how much high-end mushroom compost and horse manure this added up to. Perhaps these would turn out to be the magic ingredients to finally reverse the infertility of her apparently cursed plot.

'OK,' she muttered.

And with that we were up and running. What star-struck saddos humans are, I mused. But then, so are cats.

A week later Lucifurr, Ross and I were hiding in the tall grass in the field adjoining the allotments, watching through the wire fencing as the film crew set up on Jane's plot. On the other side of the fence, a man and a woman wearing face masks were discussing the scene about to be shot. I quickly realised the woman was the acclaimed Scandi action director Inge Marbergen while the man was Bo Leggido himself. Since he'd written the screenplay to his own Scandi noir, I didn't expect a lot of laughs. But Inge's work also involved films with high body counts, not least the seagull-themed thriller *High Squall*. I mused they'd probably end up renaming the new series *Slaughterhouse CT5*.

'I thought that perhaps we could make each of these raised beds the burial place of a victim, rather than just the one corpse as in the novel,' Bo was saying.

'Great idea – much more impact. And it's not as if the plot owner is growing anything anyway,' said Inge.

'Yes, this one here,' said Bo, stepping into a narrow bed and turning around to face in our direction, 'is perfect with that gloomy church up there on the hill with the eerie gravestones around.'

'Great idea Bo, though hang on, I think that is the plot owner's chard bed.'

'Really? I thought they were weeds,' said the writer, stepping out.

'No, they are bloody *not*,' said a steel-hard voice I knew well.

Jane strode into view in her wellingtons, pitchfork in hand, mirrored sunglasses flaring in the morning sun above her black face mask. Behind her, Grace scurried up to calm her before she impaled the Nordic clot. Words were spoken, apologies offered and just about reluctantly accepted as the level of compensation was significantly jacked up. Hands were eventually shaken and peace restored. Leggido retreated to a safe distance and started to make notes furiously, glancing furtively at Jane as she surveyed her plot, no doubt calculating how many tonnes of horse manure she could now carpet the space with. I also guessed Leggido had just discovered the model for his next all-action female fictional hero.

'God morgen,' said a chirpy high-pitched voice behind me.

The three of us turned around to face a very large and statuesque feline mountain. He had a black and white coat and the thickest fur I'd ever seen on a cat. It fell away sideways from his high tufted ears and on his white chest it widened out into a dense ruff.

Ross was the first to react. Lucifurr looked stunned, like he'd finally met his match.

'God morgen, snakker du engelsk?' Ross said.

'Yes, I speak English, as we don't have TV subtitles in Norway,' replied the vision. 'My name is Erik, which means absolute ruler, and I am a Norse Skogskatt.'

'Ahh, a Norwegian Forest Cat,' said Ross.

'And what are you doing here?' I asked.

He nodded in the direction of Bo Leggido, still scribbling furiously into his notebook.

'I'm with him, in this awful place. Why is there no snow and ice? And why is everyone so fat – don't they ski and go for long hikes? And why doesn't he speak?' he said, looking at Lucifurr.

Lucifurr was still staring at the hairy interloper but his eyes were now glinting with new confidence.

'I do more than speak,' he said in a low growl, 'and you talk too much.'

'Ah, the local Anglo-Saxon chieftain. Is this your territory?' said Erik, edging closer.

'It is.'

'Good, then we fight,' said Erik, 'and once more Viking will take this land or die trying.'

'Suits me,' said Lucifurr.

Erik leapt forward with a chirrupy squeal and the two of them rolled around in the long grass for a bit biting at each other, intertwined like snakes. Then they separated and sat taking long-distance jabs at each other's heads until, to be frank, Ross and I started getting bored. At last, as the sun started to set, exhaustion finally set in and they both dropped down into the long grass a few feet apart. The two colossi of our species smiled at each other as they licked their limbs clean and smoothed their fur.

'That was good exercise,' Erik said, 'but now I feel hungry.'

'I will show you the best hunting places in the woods. Vole, mouse, whatever you prefer,' said Lucifurr.

'Takk, det høres bra ut,' replied Erik.

'You're welcome,' said Lucifurr in a low growl.

For goodness' sake, get a bloody cat basket, I thought.

Over the following day, while Erik and Lucifurr's hunting bromance blossomed and local fauna was accordingly decimated, Ross and I continued to observe the crew filming various scenes from the long grass. The impenetrable but predictably grim Scandi plot appeared to revolve around an apparently amiable allotment holder who doubled as a serial killer and buried more than just carrot seeds under his raised beds.

The crew finished up for the day just before dusk. We watched a mechanical digger create a deep grave-shaped hole in Jane's barren asparagus plot while the cast wrapped up. Apparently, this was for the climatic shoot-out between Cooki and the killer to be filmed the following morning. This would take place around the grave and inside a stage shed that had just been plonked down by a crane in what Jane laughably called her herb patch. As we ambled home, I was still trying to decide whether the film crew had actually improved the allotment plot or not.

So it was quite a surprise to find a police tent covering the hole in the asparagus bed the following morning when we turned up to watch the cinematic shoot-out. Beside it, Jane and Alf Tennyson, her constable sidekick, were talking to Sikki Bagg, the young forensic officer, while a police photographer took pictures of the scene. A cordon had been placed encompassing several surrounding allotments, excluding various disconsolate plot holders who had been desperately trying to get themselves into shot for days. Now they were standing in a bunch behind the tape, sipping from their tea mugs.

We edged up through the long grass to the mesh fence to listen to the police chat.

'So they found the body by accident?' said Jane.

'Yes, mam,' said Alf, 'when Ms Marbergen turned up this morning she thought the grave wasn't the right depth so she got the digger back. It uncovered the body of Mr Brassica about a foot under the soil at the bottom of the hole. He was identified by a couple of plot holders who were in early. He was carrying ID as well but no keys. We think the murderer took them to get out of the gate.'

'Thank god for the social realist tradition in Scandi cinema. So, a blow to the forehead?' said Jane, turning to the forensic officer.

'Yes, likely delivered with a heavy blunt object,' said Sikki.

'Unfortunately, the place is full of them,' said Jane.

She was right. It was easy to pick up tools lying around the allotments, including spades and wood mallets.

'Do we know when he died?' asked Jane.

'Well, rigor mortis has completed so somewhere between 8 and 36 hours ago,' said Sikki.

'So he could have been killed here,' said Alf.

'Or brought here by someone who knew the grave was available,' said Jane.

'But why bring him here at all?' said Alf.

Jane did not reply. She was staring up the hillside at the gravestones surrounding the church. Behind the reflective sunglasses, I could sense a dark mood forming. Finally, she looked back at Alf.

'You all right, Mam?' he said.

Jane started and looked down quickly.

'Fine. Just remembering an old unsolved case, but more importantly wondering if I'll still get paid for the allotment. Let's get on with interviewing the actors and film crew – indeed anyone who was here yesterday.'

They glanced across at the huddle of plot holders behind the cordon. The muddy-sweatered rabble perked up and waved their tea mugs to attract the female detective's attention.

'Oy Jane, the weather's turning and I need to get my onions out!' shouted one.

'And my Pink Fir Apple spuds won't last either!' boomed another.

'What about my marrows – they need cutting back as well,' lobbed in a third.

'All heart and dirty wellies,' muttered Jane.

I saw Alf roll his eyes.

'Well, September is the start of the gardening year,' said Sikki brightly, looking around, 'and this plot could certainly do with a fresh start.'

Jane lowered her glasses and gave Sikki a cold ice-blue stare that just about turned her to stone, before turning back to Alf.

'And dig up everything you can on Broderic Brassica.'

'Yes, mam. No pun intended I'm sure,' replied Alf.

And once more we were off. I only hoped the police would

be some help to me in solving this one. But I wasn't holding my breath.

One thing I was sure about from the start was that this was a formulaic Scandi murder. To solve it I would need to look in gloomy urban places or wild open landscapes, be alert to social commentary about the slow breakdown of the post-war welfare state and to sudden illogical links to old unsolved cold cases. There would probably also be a bit of odd behaviour by an aged character, a millionaire entrepreneur with a kinky penchant or three, a local politician found dead in a shipping container and a hell of lot of moody staring out at the cold grey sea. Well, I could do the last of those at the end when the credits rolled, but it was the bits in-between I needed to get to grips with. Especially as the plot would have more holes in it than an Icelandic fishing trawler's net.

I thought we'd start with the millionaire, so I asked Ross to comb the local press and online chatter for local dodgy entrepreneurial activity. Meanwhile, I checked out how the allotments fitted in with what passes for the welfare state locally.

I discovered to my surprise after trawling the council website and making some fraudulent Freedom of Information requests from Grace's iPad, that the allotments were on the empty sloping burial land below St Hengist's church. It had been used by land girls to produce potatoes during WWII. After the war the then-progressive council had determined that the western slope of Seaview Hill would never be required for graves and had turned the land into allotments. Generations of whelkies had then struggled with the unyielding clay soil, the eternal bindweed and immortal carrot fly in order to present their families with something that resembled a comestible plant. But at least the sea view when they lifted their eyes from the interminable weeding was always stunning. So, tick off the wild open landscape.

More recently, the growth in the retirement population of the town had resulted in a slow advance by the untidy army of gravestones around the church towards the allotments, as ever more old-timers popped their clogs. There had been whisperings in recent years that the council might have to take the land back, with the allotments moved inland to other council fields, but nothing had come of it. I was assured in the reply to one of my FoI requests that there were 'no plans at present to change current arrangements'. Hmm, I'd thought – what does 'no plans at present' mean?

Ross and I met at Cape Cataveral later that afternoon. He had news of his own.

'"Wild Hog" Fenella Kincaid is in town,' he said without preamble.

'What?' I miaowed.

As far as I knew, burlesque artist and rap DJ 'Wild Hog' Fenella, entrepreneur matriarch and brains of my mortal enemies the Kincaid crime clan, had been licking her wounds in Stoke Newington following the arrest and imprisonment of her husband 'Pop' Kincaid and their son, Billy. I had managed to get them both sent down after exposing the Whitstable postcard case, but had not succeeded in entangling the clan's *capa* in my crime-busting coup.

'There has to be a link to this murder,' I said.

'I agree it seems to fit the Scandi formula,' said Ross, 'but there's no obvious link to allotments.'

'Nevertheless, that's the kinky millionaire bit ticked off,' I answered.

The next link seemed to come at dawn the following morning, when Runa Bean opened the allotment's container store and discovered local councillor and allotment lessee Kelda Quick under the rotavator. Unfortunately, the rotavator had been used on her, so all Runa saw was a rather chomped-up mess which was only identified several hours later. The telephone call to Jane came in just as she was about leave the house, and I overheard the whole conversation with Alf Tennyson.

Twenty minutes later, Ross and I were once more lying in the undergrowth behind the wire fence only a few feet from the open shipping container, listening to Jane, Alf and Sikki discussing the murder.

'Tick corpse in container,' whispered Ross.

'Shut up and listen,' I hissed.

Jane was questioning the forensics officer.

'So when do we think it happened?' she said.

'Well, from the condition of the body, I'd say the middle of last night,' said Sikki.

'Bloody noisy, rotavators,' said Jane.

'Blood spatter on the container walls suggests the container door was closed,' said Sikki.

'Which explains why no one around remembers hearing the rotavator sound,' added Alf.

'Why was Runa Bean trying to use it so early?' said Jane.

'Ahh, Mam, that's her guilty secret. Turns out they are not

189

all no-dig on that plot after all. They churn up the clay a bit in their beds as well and add their hippy manure before they put their Algerian turnips in.'

'Tut, tut,' said Sikki, 'that is naughty.'

'I knew it!' said Jane, a twist of schadenfreude playing on her lips. 'Well, they'll never live it down. Any other clues?'

'We've managed to salvage Councillor Quick's mobile, Mam. I've had a look through it. You'll want to see this video,' said Alf.

He held up the phone inside its clear plastic evidence bag to Jane's face and pressed the screen. I could just hear some squealing and raucous shouting coming from the phone.

'Oh dear,' said Jane, 'my poor asparaguses sacrificed for this.'

I sat on the lounge windowsill pretending to look out at the rain while Jane gave Grace the juicy details.

'Well, I've heard of people who like doing it in graveyards, but down in a grave takes the biscuit,' said Grace.

'Well, it was only a stage grave, actually,' said Jane.

'Leggido only married last year.'

'Yes, to that dodgy Kazakh billionaire's daughter. Certainly gives him a motive to do Brassica in before step-daddy found out.'

'So you think Broderic stumbled across them and filmed them?'

'I know he did. He mailed the video to his friend councillor Quick that night, probably just before he ended up in the grave,' said Jane.

'Why didn't she inform the authorities when we found his body?'

'Perhaps she saw a profitable once-in-a-lifetime blackmail opportunity,' said Jane.

'Sounds far-fetched. Why did Marbergen ask for the grave to be dug deeper the following morning?'

'We think Leggido did Broderic in after she'd left the allotment and then buried him alone – we don't think Marbergen was involved or knew about it.'

'And then what? Quick sees a blackmail opportunity, meets Leggido the following night and gets rotavated?' said Grace.

'Works for me,' said Jane, 'that's why we are questioning both of them.'

'What are they saying?'

'Not a lot apart from claiming innocence. Oh, and that I'm not getting my allotment rental fee.'

Looking out at a couple of blackbirds, I wasn't buying it. Of course, human sexual behaviour was always weird for cats. For us, the female always decides where and when. As soon as the dirty is done we give the male a swipe round the chops and tell him to get lost. Two months later out pops the litter. It's quick, efficient and to the point.

First, there was no proof that Leggido and Marbergen had even noticed Brassica, or if they had that they minded. For some humans half the thrill is getting spotted doing it al fresco. Second, it beggared belief that Councillor Quick would meet up with Leggido in the middle of the night in a sealed container if she suspected he was a murderer. Even a local councillor is not that thick. Third, any half-competent blackmail victim would have taken the phone and deleted the video after doing the deed.

But most of all, it didn't fit the Scandi noir formula. We were still missing the odd aged characters with the crucial insight and the illogical cold case link. No, the two mucky lovers were being fitted up like a couple of muddy kippers.

I assembled the team later that morning at Cape Cataveral, including Erik, who was distraught at the arrest of his owner. He scoffed at the idea that Bo would have murdered anyone for witnessing a bit of six-foot-under action.

'That is such a repressed British crime story narrative,' he said haughtily.

'Agreed,' I answered, 'but how do we prove it?'

'Well,' said Lucifurr, 'we were hunting on the allotment the night of the first murder. We didn't hear any commotion.'

Ross and I turned to each other in shock. I rounded back on Lucifurr.

'And you didn't think to mention this earlier, you oversized fur-ball?'

'There was nothing to report, and we were busy killing for sport,' said Erik defensively.

I shook my head. It made sense, sort of. The allotments were basically a large buffet table laid out by humans for local voles, mice, rabbits, snails, birds, you name the species. Erik interrupted my musings with his Nordic moaning.

'If Bo isn't cleared, I may never swim across the fjords, bask in the midnight sun and the northern lights, hunt once more in the deep snow...'

'Shut up, you hairy lump, I'm thinking,' I hissed.

The Norwegian cat mountain harrumphed but didn't complain. Well, they never do, do they? Finally, I looked back at the feeble-minded pair.

'Describe anything you saw in the allotments that was unusual,' I said.

'Well, there was Pètr of course, but he's always there late at night, talking to his vegetables,' said Lucifurr.

Yes, of course, old Pètr, or 'Downhill Petey' as he was better known to the other allotment lessees, had the largest plot, right at the bottom of Seaview Hill. He operated it using the open-field system. Also a reputed member of the local Kentish druidic society, he knew his onions, literally.

'Anything else?' I said.

'Well, just some bloke filling up the water butts. All except Petey's, that is,' said Lucifurr.

'Not strange at all, then,' said Ross caustically.

'No, it is quite dry for the time of year,' said Erik.

I stared at the muscle mountains for a bit.

'You two are made for each other,' I said.

'Err, thanks,' said Lucifurr.

I turned to Ross.

'What about you?'

'Well, the big news is that the council is taking back the allotments.'

'Yikes!' I yowled.

'Yes, they've found pollution in the soil in the allotments. They think it's been contaminated by the groundwater carrying contaminants from the graves at the top of the hill. It's called necroleachate, but then there's also the embalming fluids, the formaldehyde, which is a carcinogenic, and various other nasties, like the cobalt in fillings and implants and the varnishes and preservatives in coffins. Frankly, you don't want to know the details.'

'Holy Bastet,' I gasped.

'Yes, human graveyards are basically landfill, if you think about it. This one seems to have leaked. The heavy clay soil retains the water running downhill. So they are going to move the allotments, clean up the soil and then build on it.'

There was a loud retching sound. We looked across to see Erik vomiting onto the pine needles. Lucifurr also looked decidedly nauseous, but was somehow managing to gag it back.

'We've been hunting a lot on the allotments,' he said at last.

'Eating loads of animals who feed on those poisoned vegetables,' groaned Erik.

I was unimpressed by the drama. Both of them looked pretty healthy to me. I nodded over at a clump of tall grass by the fence.

'Best get chewing, then,' I said.

I turned back to Ross.

'When was all this decided?'

'Last week, but just announced. No doubt the murders are a good excuse to get the news out.'

'No doubt indeed,' I purred.

At last the various Scandi noir pieces were moving together. But I still had a visit to make to one of them.

It was midnight when I found Downhill Petey sitting in his cracked plastic chair, singing softly to his root vegetables under a crescent moon. I sat next to the old man just as he finished his chant and lifted his ale bottle to his lips for a long swig. He threw his head back, the round cauliflower ears and misshapen tuber nose pale in the moonlight, eyes closed and Adam's apple twitching as he sucked down the dregs. Finally, he straightened, belched and placed the empty bottle down by the chair leg, turning to me as he did so.

'Hello at last, little one. Pardon my drinking, I'm in fakement today,' he said.

I looked at him. Could he really have been expecting me?

'Yes, I was,' he said smiling, 'ever since we were told that the allotments are to be closed, I've been sitting here awaiting you.'

Well, tick odd, aged character, I thought.

'No offence taken. I'm in 'opes you can save this sacred place,' he said, drunkenly throwing his right arm out in a protective arc.

I scratched the soil with my paw and looked at him.

'That's a LIE!' he roared, fighting to stand up from his chair, 'us longtails have been planting this land since afore the Romans and certainly long before them scrumped upstarts!'

I followed the direction of his outstretched finger. It was pointing at the silhouette of St Hengist's church tower.

'You see, little one, there's secrets buried deep beneath my rhubarb which must never be revealed,' he said.

I looked at the soil again. I needed more.

'You don't believe me – you think me an old nisy, no doubt, but it's that nabbler Brassica you ought to investigate. Scaddling around at night with his water jugs.'

He dropped back into the cracked plastic chair with a thump.

'Look now,' he said, pointing his arm over his allotment, ancient fingers outstretched.

I looked over the ridged clay before us. Imperceptibly at first, the light of the moon increased, covering the ground in a pale blue glow. And then I saw them, in their dozens, over what seemed like hours. The shrews, the wood mice and the moles, the swooping tawny owls and pipistrelles, the rabbits, earthworms and foxes. And everywhere around them, in their thousands, the ground beetles, devil's coach horses and earwigs. And so many more, all doing their thing amidst the bowing blackberry and raspberry bushes and the ripe tomatoes, marrows and courgettes.

When at last my eyes were completely sated, Downhill Petey slowly lowered his hand and the darkness crept back in over the plots.

'Do any of them look peaky to you, little friend?' he said.

No, of course not, I thought.

He smiled down at me and stroked my head, scratching under my ears, which was lovely.

'You know, I've never liked nosy coppers like your Jane, but I'll do you a scoase – a deal,' he said.

He didn't need to spell it out. I was already on my way.

Jane was standing at the kitchen worktop preparing the evening meal – an elaborate vegetarian roast. She sliced through the perfect potatoes and onions that Downhill Petey had insisted on giving her on her last visit to her plot and sighed with envy. Grace had opened another bottle of Riesling and was filling the two glasses. Ross and I stood by our bowls

196

listening for the news.

'Thanks hon,' said Jane, stopping for a moment to take a swig.

'So it's all wrapped up then?' said Grace.

'Yup, almost, and all thanks to Downhill Petey really.'

'I can't believe the scale of it.'

'Well, it was all about following the money and working out who benefitted from the allotments being developed.'

'And then you saw that profile of "Wild Hog" Fenella Kincaid in *Whitstable Whisperer* magazine, all about her looking for local development opportunities. Genius really – you are so clever!'

Ross and I looked at each other. We'd dragged that bloody profile around the house for days, leaving the mag open on the sofa, the coffee table and the bedroom, until we'd almost yowled in despair. It was only when we'd left it in the loo that she'd picked it up to read. Human thought really is closely related to crap.

'Then it was just a matter of tracing it back. Kincaid's many dinners with Quick in the Swearbox and long boozy lunches in the Ancient Poseidon came to light quickly, as did Quick's intensive secretive lobbying in various committees to take the allotments back and carry out soil analysis,' said Jane.

'But how did you make the link to Broderic Brassica?'

'I always thought Brassica was dodgy. When his predecessor, Knut Calabrese, died last year after falling unexpectedly off his experimental oversized Hügelkultur mound, Brassica fell briefly under suspicion. But we couldn't prove anything as Knut's body was missing from his grave when we finally got permission to carry out a post-mortem toxicology report. But Downhill Petey gave us the vital clues.'

'You mean telling you about the empty water butts?

'That too. He rang to tell us all the butts Brassica had been topping up had been emptied overnight. I told him to immediately stop the plot holders re-filling. Nearly caused a riot, mind.'

'I still can't believe Brassica was poisoning the water in the butts. Or that Kincaid was stupid enough to empty them all.'

Well, not quite, Sherlock, I said to myself. We'd worked out that once the decision to take the allotments back had been agreed, Kincaid had every incentive to kill her confederates off to keep them quiet. Brassica's voyeurism had given her the perfect opportunity to take them out and pin it on Leggido. We just needed to convince her that she'd been seen.

So Ross had managed to get Kincaid to come back to the allotments in the dead of night to meet and kill the anonymous blackmailer who had sent her an untraceable email detailing her involvement. She'd spent a fruitless night waiting in the container before leaving nonplussed towards dawn.

Meanwhile Lucifurr and Erik had spent the night racing around the allotments pushing open the taps on 187 water butts. It was the least they could do in the circumstances and a rare example of them using their thick heads. When the police had turned up the following morning and tested the ground beneath the butts and the bottom residues inside them they had found all the fake necroleachate they needed.

'Or stupid enough to leave her prints on the gate lock,' said Grace.

That was a happy bonus. Kincaid had forgotten that due to Covid rules the plot holders had to wear gloves to open the gate lock. She'd used Brassica's key to get in and out but having committed no crime that night she'd been careless leaving the allotments. Not that it would have mattered. I'd taken stake-out pictures of her entering and leaving the container on Grace's GoPro camera which would have found their way into Jane's inbox. But this way was better – our handiwork was completely invisible.

'And you solved your cold case as well!' said Grace.

'Again, Downhill Pete gave me the clue. When I spoke to him about Knut's sad demise and his empty grave he asked me if I knew that the coffins often drift downhill if the graves are not dug deep enough. Downhill creep, it's called. So we dug again a few feet downhill and there was Knut's coffin. Ready to yield its own murderous story, I'm sure.'

Yes, tick old cold case off the Scandi formula.

'So all you need to do now is to catch "Wild Hog" Fenella Kincaid,' said Grace.

Jane nodded and re-started chopping Petey's vegetables. When Kincaid's sea view apartment in Tankerton had been raided they'd found she'd left in a hurry. Someone in the know had warned her.

'Oh, she won't get far. We've frozen her assets and the ports and airports are on high alert for her. When we do get her the evidence of her bribing Quick and Brassica is strong,' said Jane.

Yes, the Kincaid empire was done. But I would not relax until the nipple-tassel spinning crime dominatrix who had bestridden the local crime scene was in the slammer. Yes, the allotments' buried secrets had been saved for another millennium or two, the Scandi noir filming had resumed on them, Lucifurr and Erik were decimating local small mammals again and the downhill-drifting corpse had been located, but there was always an unexpected, twisted sequel with someone like 'Wild Hog' Fenella Kincaid.

Eventually, our sozzled 'owners' remembered we were there and fed us. After I'd finished cleaning myself I realised there was something left to do. I crept out of the cat flap and crossed the quiet roads and fields until I was at the boundary of St Hengist's church graveyard, looking into the allotments. I found the concealed gap in the wire fencing and crept towards Downhill Petey's plot. He was nowhere to be seen. I jumped onto one of the rainfall-catching water butts backing onto his small shed and then hopped up onto the felt roof. I surveyed the rich magnificence of his crops and remembered with a smile his silent promise to transform Jane's miserable mud plot into a similar Garden of Eden. But I was not there to speculate on the buried power that fuelled the fertility of this Kentish patch of ground.

I was there to stare moodily out at the sea's calm surface, which reflected the flaring purples and ochres of another stirring Whelkville sunset. Not cold and grey like in another tedious Scandi noir ending, but hey, who gives a shit.

Tick.

10

A Windy Ending To A Wave Of
Whitstable Terror

IT WAS EARLY OCTOBER AND THE MOOD IN THE TOWN WAS ON the slide. Covid cases had been rising for weeks and everyone knew in their hearts that a second lockdown was probably only weeks away. Meanwhile, the police had utterly failed to track down 'Wild Hog' Fenella Kincaid. The local press was in uproar and Jane and Alf wore increasingly grim expressions as the criticism mounted.

To make matters worse, a low-level crimewave had engulfed the town. Some even suspected that from some unknown lair the Kincaid *capa del capi* had instigated a vengefully mean assault upon Whitstable. Anyone writing a letter to the local press condemning the open daylight sweets theft from a local supermarket was likely to find their wheelie bins had been viciously tipped over. When the manager of the supermarket in question was interviewed to bewail this criminality, she found the next day that all the lipsticks on display had been opened, used and replaced on the shelves.

After this outrage, councillor Hedda Linechase, who'd promised to get more coppers on the streets of the cowering town, found that her letterbox had been superglued shut and her front garden terracotta pots cruelly emptied of their over-composted contents. The unstated message of this intimidation was clear. Get used to this, sucker, it's the new normal.

When local Chief Constable Rob Ottick asserted on Whitstable Shore Radio that this outrageous wave of intimidation could not be allowed to persist, his front and rear car number plates were nicked and hung from the Duke of Cumbria pub sign. Whelkville had known nothing like it for generations. Thefts of valuables from cars also continued at a high level, but everyone agreed that those still leaving handbags, phones and designer dogs in plain view after years of crime prevention advice deserved everything they got.

What was unclear was what the instigators of this wave of small-scale criminality hoped to gain from this deluge of wrongdoing, but the effect on the town's morale was marked. Already foreseeing the restoration of restrictive measures on their freedoms, the citizenry now also had to worry about low level pilfering, unforeseen driveway littering and the desecration of their front flower beds. Frantic twitching of net curtains and fancy blinds by residents as strangers passed by reached unparalleled heights.

The mood was turning ugly. But none of us cats guessed things were about to get much worse.

The full reign of terror was unleashed a few days later. The

Tankerton citizenry awoke to find the whole frontage of their famously colourful beach huts near Long Rock spray-painted black. On the door of each darkened beach hut a five-foot high letter was sprayed in brilliant white. Collectively they spelt out a grim warning:

'BEGONE TANCRED'S PEOPLE – YOUR TIME HAS COME!'

The police recovered dozens of black and white spray cans from the scene but remained at a loss about who was responsible. Early howls of anger directed at local youths were disabused when it was pointed out no local teenager was likely to know that the word Tancred was the origin of Tankerton's name, but much more importantly, there were no spelling errors.

Two days later, as the town struggled to recover from the Two-Tone Tankerton Terror, as the *Kentish Digest* had dubbed it, it was Seasalter's turn. The sewage pumping station serving the caravan parks around the Seasalter Levels and nearby beachside homes was broken into at night and vandalised. The large quantity of sea salt dropped into the wet well jammed up the pump, forcing sewage back into surrounding homes and caravans. Chaos ensued, with caravan owners fleeing the holiday parks as their toilet pans projectile-vomited sewage. A local health and safety emergency was declared.

A grim graffiti message greeted Jane and Alf on their arrival outside of the pumping station:

'EAT SHIT, SEASALTER STAYCATIONERS!'

'What do you think they will hit next?' asked Ross.

'I don't know,' I said, sounding feeble even to myself.

Lucifurr, Ross and I were having our daily COBRA (Cats Only Briefing Report & Analysis) meeting on Cape Cataveral in the Crab & Winkle undergrowth. A few yards away, behind the wood fencing we could hear Jane being calmed down by Grace, following another fruitless day in the 'Wild Hog' Fenella inquiry and no luck identifying the local vandals. This involved Grace plying Jane with large volumes of single malt.

'It looks like economic disruption, hitting the cultural mainstays of the town. Seems inevitable that it will be Whitstable after Tankerton and Seasalter. But where, I couldn't tell you,' I said.

'In that case they will strike another tourist magnet,' said Lucifurr.

'What fits the bill?' I said.

'The huts on West Beach?' ventured Ross.

'Too well guarded,' said Lucifurr. 'I can barely get down there for my daily swim now for all the dog patrols the hut owners are doing.'

'I agree, and it's also too predictably a repeat of the Two-Tone Tankerton Terror,' I said.

'The Ancient Poseidon pub by the beach perhaps then,' said Ross.

'Too many plain-clothes coppers and DFLs hanging around at all hours looking obvious and taking terrible photos respectively,' I said.

We similarly dismissed the recently built luxury pads overlooking the shore (guarded by a rotating posse of local estate agents), the Swearbox restaurant (now protected by a fleet of encircling mini-tractors and in any instance also closely monitored by the ever-present Preservation Alliance of Whitstable (PAW)). And finally, we ruled out the Whelkbridge arts centre, which was presently under another undeserved siege from local repeat-offender demonstrators.

'What are they demonstrating about now?' I asked, out of interest.

'Nothing. Just keeping their hand in until something comes up, so we think they will just go on being outraged till they drop dead,' said Ross.

'We are missing something here,' I said, 'what about CCTV?'

'Jane told Grace that they have no record of suspicious activity on the roads leading to Tankerton slopes or near the Seasalter caravan parks. She and Alf are completely stumped,' said Ross.

I lay down on my back on the grass covering of Cape Cataveral and rolled from one side to the other.

'Back itch?' said Lucifurr.

'Yep – and it helps me think.'

'So what next?' said Ross.

'Well, I'd normally say use median centre spatial location, like you used to identify the crime lair of the limbless catalytic burglars, but I don't suppose you have enough information for that?' I said.

'No, sadly,' said Ross. 'I'd need a few more data points.'

'OK, in that case can you carry out a detailed econometric analysis of Whitstable's economy, taking into account...'

Ross's eyes were lighting up.

'...gross value-added, retail sales, employment, property

values,' he interrupted.

'Yes, that way we might be able to predict the next economic target.'

'That's brilliant,' both my partners in crime-busting chime-miaowed.

'Well – that's why I'm here,' I said modestly.

While Ross hacked the district council's system to obtain the data needed to plug into his economic model, Lucifurr and I headed down into Whelkville to pick up anecdotal micro-economic evidence to add to the analysis. Slipping down that evening into the centre via an overgrown and forgotten sailor's alley, we soon saw the signs of business armageddon. The estate agents' windows were teeming with knock-down house sales and slashed staycation rental prices. Indeed, many of the rental properties were also up for sale. The restaurants, chip shops and pubs were bereft of locals and DFLs. The former were probably guarding their flower beds and allotments while the latter had actually started observing the restrictions. You know things are bad when the well-heeled middle-classes start following the rules.

Whitstable's new status as the economic crime and mindless vandalism capital of the North Kent coast had blown an ill wind through its streets and alleys. Indeed, we barely saw anyone as we made our way through Harbour Street. On the whitewashed sidewall of one building the town's graffitist, Moggsy, had sprayed a giant tumbleweed made up of entwined tiny people blowing through a background of boarded-up shops. Genius as ever.

'I can't believe all this has happened so quickly,' said Lucifurr.

'When podgy blond bumbler brings in the next lockdown, that'll be the *coup de...*'

I was interrupted by the dull roar of an explosion ahead of us. A moment later we heard screams and a whole cacophony of alarms going off.

'What the...' said Lucifurr.

'Of course,' I gasped, 'the harbour!'

We raced towards the car park at the entrance to the port, then slipped like shadows between the piles of nets and lobster pots lining the quays until we reached a group of fishermen looking towards the harbour entrance. It was high tide, and for a moment, amidst the peal of sirens and horns, with the disturbed water still slapping the top of the wooden harbour walls and the wildly bobbing red and blue fishing boats, all was chaos.

'They've sunk 'er!' one of them groaned.

I looked across at the only large ship resting against the East Quay, the mighty *Sea Uranus,* which brought the weekly supply of granite blocks and sand to the looming Whelky Setts Paving plant that so defined the town. On the length of her dark hull someone had sprayed their ominous terror message in enormous capitals:

'WHELKLESS YOU WILL DIE, WHITSTABLE!'

I could see three large holes beneath the waterline on the starboard side of the *Sea Uranus.* They were filling fast, spewing forth the remaining air from the ship's interior as they did so in bubbling water cascades. I knew in an instant the ship was mortally stricken. Men and cats stood watching her slowly list over, spilling some of her stony load across the harbour entrance as she settled. Then, at last, she came to rest, twisted over on the sediment below the muddied water. The fishermen beside us removed their woolly hats to pay her silent homage while the hooter on the top of the plant's bucket elevator tooted out a long mournful note.

I could see that only a thin channel of water out of the harbour remained between the carcass of the *Sea Uranus* and the West Quay opposite her. Too narrow now for the squat oyster fishing boats and whelkers to squeeze through, I realised. I had the same pit-of-the-stomach feeling as when Ross advanced a piece on Grace's chessboard and said 'check' in a neutral tone, only magnified a hundred times. Check for the town's fishing and garden paving industries. But hopefully not quite mate for the town.

The emergency services started to arrive almost immediately, ambulances and fire engines screeching to a halt on the East Quay, adding to the general din. We slipped away back through the plastic crates and lobster pots before more locals arrived and finally noticed us.

'So, it's total economic war,' I muttered to myself as we retreated up the hill to our home overlooking the stricken town.

An eerie calm descended on Whelkville after sinking of the *Sea Uranus,* which had paralysed the Whelky Setts plant and bottled in the town's fishing fleet for the foreseeable. With the DFLs now completely scared off, the town's restaurant and

208

pointless knick-knack shops culture had been decimated. The town's fish and chip shops, including Flossie's, were only kept afloat by the regular deliveries of Cornish fish, and the arrival of the refrigerated lorries bringing in the cod was greeted like the 1948 Berlin air-drops. But once they collected their cod and chips of an evening the citizenry retreated home to protect their bins and plant pots or to stand guard in Home Guard-like platoons beside their allotments and beach huts. Whelkville had been well and truly blitzed.

The following day, our COBRA meeting was a sombre affair. Ross dolefully recited the economic statistics and we debated possible ways of identifying the next target. It was a grey windy day and above us the trees swayed, disgorging yellowing leaves to the ground with every gust.

'What we really need is a balanced recovery,' I said.

'Well, we have a relatively old population. For example, 10% of Swalies and Tankies are over 80, but mostly quite affluent, so it will need to be consumption-led,' said Ross.

'We also have lots of locals on low incomes who need better paying secure jobs, as well as plenty of children living in poverty. Are we going to solve that as well?' asked Lucifurr.

'I agree – keep it simple. So we need a recovery in tourism and retail, fuelled by DFL money if possible,' replied Ross, missing the hint.

Ross's mind always works in straight lines of least resistance, so I didn't hold his classical free-market approach against him. But we needed a more activist approach rooted in behavioural economics.

'No, I've been thinking about this and the same old same old will not do. What the town needs is a transformational Miaowshall Plan whereby the supply of the most valued goods in town is owned in common. What provides the greatest value-added in town?'

Ross shook his head for a bit. But then that's how he gets the neurons working.

'Well, I suppose whelks, sea-front accommodation including the beach-huts, and of course knick-knack and postcard sales,' he answered.

'In the 19th century the freemen of the Company of Free Whelkers had a local monopoly of whelk fishing, and they looked after the families of the whelkers and the wider community. So all we need to do is to...' I started.

Lucifurr interjected with a low miaow of frustration. I looked across at him stretched out with his front paws resting on the trunk of a tree. He lacerated the bark, one paw after another, not looking at us.

'Our job is to solve crimes, not create a Whelkville industrial strategy for these bozos who can't get it together,' he intoned darkly.

His words hit me like a train. What was I doing getting us involved in the town's economic recovery? Our job was to catch whoever was committing these dark deeds. I lay on the ground and stared at the fallen leaves around us. The wind was getting stronger and we cats don't like stormy days. It was time to go indoors and get a hold of myself. When had I started thinking like a biped?

'Perhaps there won't be any more attacks,' said Ross. 'After all, by wrecking the holiday accommodation and ruining the town's whelking and garden paving industries, the place has been brought to its knees. No one is buying the Whitstable sunset paintings at Chattels or postcards of boats bobbing in the harbour.'

'No, I can sense in my whiskers that this isn't over,' I said.

Lucifurr stopped grooming his shiny black fur and spoke again.

'When I have a mouse trapped, I play with it for a bit, biting off a bit of tail, perhaps an ear, before I chew its head off. That's what this feels like.'

'What about its legs?'

'That would be unsporting. Got to let it run around in terror for a bit.'

We nodded. Lucifurr was on form today.

'It's true that everything that's happened is temporary. The beach huts will be cleaned up and the pumping station will be repaired. Even the *Sea Uranus* will eventually be floated and the harbour dredged of its spilled load,' I said.

'So we are looking for a knock-out punch?' said Ross.

I looked at him. The wind was rising to a howl, pushing his tabby fur flat to his sides.

'Yes, we need to do some more digging, and quick,' I said.

🐈

It was late and Ross and I were working in the study. Jane was on duty while Grace had gone to beddy-byes after polishing off a passable Cabernet. We wouldn't be disturbed for hours. Out there in the raging storm that now gripped the town Lucifurr was scouting the abandoned streets looking for clues of a possible further outrage. I didn't envy him his paw leather duties.

On the desktop, Ross was researching economic catastrophes that had wiped out human habitation through the ages while I investigated recent unusual crimes on the

211

police database on Grace's iPad. He'd ruled out plague, volcanic eruption, invasion and rapid climate change, while I'd also drawn a blank with rural crimes involving livestock, large-scale arson and local overpriced car parks.

Then, simultaneously, as if guided by some unknown feline spirit, we both speeded up our searching and reading, clicking and flicking over web pages like demons until we both sat back and looked at one another.

'Flooding,' he said.

'Explosives,' I countered.

'WHAT THE F***!?' we both yowled in unison.

Ross was the first to recover.

'The town was nearly wiped out in 1953 by a flood. Low air pressure, a storm surge and strong winds combined to submerge the town. But look...'

He pointed at his screen. It showed a mass of weather information and a map of the sea off Whitstable. A series of arrows on screen had aimed themselves at the North Kent coast while various isobar lines were centred around a depression in the sea close to the town.

'A storm surge is coming down the coast, and the wind is blowing anti-clockwise around that depression. Looks bad but it should be nothing to really worry about,' he said.

'Why not?' I said.

'Well, the town's anti-flood defences are much stronger now than in '53.'

'What if we are wrong?'

'How could we be wrong?' he said.

We heard a crunching in the kitchen as the locked cat flap was once more torn from its hinges by our muscle-bound confederate. A few moments later Lucifurr padded into the study, his fur slick from the driving rain. He collapsed onto the rug and lay there breathing hard.

'Something's wrong,' he gasped, 'some of the floodgates on West Beach have been opened up.'

'How is that possible?' I miaowed.

'Well, the weather is so bad there's no one around to stop it,' replied Lucifurr.

'High tide is around 3am,' said Ross, 'but even then any flooding should only be an inconvenience not a disaster.'

'What if the tidal surge waves were boosted?'

It was Ross's turn to look alarmed.

'How?'

'Let me show you what I found,' I said.

I manoeuvred the iPad around on the rug and we clustered around it.

'Three weeks ago, recreational divers explored the wreck of the *S.S. Moggytomery* off the coast of Sheerness. Though this was strictly forbidden, they made an alarming discovery,' I said.

'The *Moggytomery*? The sunken WWII Liberty ship with all the explosives onboard?' said Ross.

'No longer. The divers found all the explosives had been removed by persons unknown.'

Ross and Lucifurr's tails puffed up involuntarily.

'What on earth is anyone going to do with old WWII munitions?' said Lucifurr.

'Build a tsunami bomb, of course!' miaowed Ross in a high squeak.

'What on earth is a tsunami bomb?' I gasped.

'There was a programme called "Project Seal", developed by the US and New Zealand during WWII, to lay explosives on the sea floor to produce tsunamis that would devastate coastal defences in Japan,' said Ross.

'So we think that someone is going to detonate a bunch of old explosives off Whitstable to help flood it out?' said Lucifurr.

'Perfectly disguised by the high tide and the storm,' I said, 'so it would look as if the Met Office had miscalculated the storm surge.'

'But how would they detonate them in a raging storm?' said Lucifurr.

'Easy peasy,' said Ross, who had already flicked through the relevant pages of his online *Encyclopaedia Britannicatica,* 'It's a command wire IED, so they'd just need an electric firing cable and a power source.'

'But there are no ships out there in this weather,' I said.

Ross had already brought up a live feed marine map off Whitstable on-screen. He glanced at me and smiled, then we all looked down at the blue grid squares.

Lucifurr spoke first.

'Too risky to run the line ashore, the Red Forts are too far out and have no power, so...'

'It can't be...' I said, in shock.

'It bloody well is,' said Lucifurr.

We looked at the neatly arranged rows of dots on the map, just a few miles offshore. Not just a power source but a bloody great generator.

The Flattish Kent Array wind farm.Of course.

'But which turbine has the firing cable?' I said.

'Probably the one with the lift for VIP visits. Our tsunami bomber will want to be up there to gauge when the tide and the storm are at their height before setting off the explosives,'

214

replied Ross.

'We've got to alert the authorities,' said Lucifurr, 'we can't handle this ourselves.'

If cats could laugh or cry I wouldn't have known which to do. An anonymous email to the local cops claiming that a terrorist on a wind turbine was going to blow up WWII munitions stolen from a sunken merchantman to cause a tsunami and drown the town would probably not get priority treatment. We needed someone who would believe us. Once more Lucifurr proved he was more than cat-brawn.

'What about Captain Rack Jackham of the *Perky Pecker*?'

Ross and I looked at our partner-in-crime-busting in open admiration. It was genius. Captain Jackham had been restoring the tiny 19th century whelker boat in a corner of the harbour for what seemed like years. The descendant of a long line of Seasalter pirates and smugglers, he'd certainly believe this criminal caper might be true.

Lucifurr went on.

'It's the only vessel in the harbour that can get out there to the turbines. She's fully restored, a mere three-foot draft, small engine installed for chartering, though she'll probably sail out through the waves under a storm jib...'

'How do you know all this shit?' miaowed Ross.

'I'm the official ship's cat,' Lucifurr replied. 'I'm the great-great-great-great-grandson of Unsinkable Sam.'

Ross and I purred in appreciation. Unsinkable Sam! Who'd survived the sinking of the *Bismark*, the destroyer HMS *Cossack* and then HMS *Ark Royal*. No wonder Lucifurr liked a swim.

Time was tight and we threw ourselves back into the work that needed to be done. I drafted the anonymous email to

Rack Jackham while Ross assembled a file of circumstantial evidence on the case to attach to it. He included underwater pictures of the empty hold of the *Moggytomery* and detailed calculations demonstrating conclusively that the wave the explosion would create on the Whitstable shore would be ten feet high. Ten minutes later Ross pressed 'send' and the three of us slipped through the cat flap into the stormy night.

By the time we reached the harbour we knew it had worked. Rack Jackham and his live-in lovers and restoration volunteers, Mary Bonney and Anny Ready, were on deck in their waterproofs, frantically readying the *Perky Pecker* for sailing as the rain poured down. I could hear the small engine chugging beneath the clinker boats' timbers. Ross and I hid behind the lobster pots but Lucifurr leapt straight down into the boat from the dockside.

'Lucifurr!' I yowled. I emerged from my hiding place and looked down at the whelker's deck. Lucifurr had landed behind Rack Jackham and was looking back up at me. He seemed quite unaffected by the bobbing of the boat.

Jackham turned around and burst into laughter.

'Look girls, our lucky Hemingway cat is here – he'll keep us safe!'

Hemingway cat, I thought, amidst the driving rain.

'What about that one?'

I looked across to see Mary Bonney pointing up at me on the dock.

'Must be his bit of stuff, Mary,' laughed Anny Ready, 'here to see him off!'

Bloody cheek, I thought. And without any forethought I launched myself down off the dock. I landed on the deck with a damp thud and a sharp realisation of having just done something really dumb. I looked up at the dock and saw Ross's eyes peeking out between the lobster pots.

Too bleeding late now.

'Bloody hell,' said Mary, 'she must be keen, the little ginger trollop.'

There was no time for further repartee as at that moment Rack cast us off and the boat moved out of its berth and turned to edge along the harbour wall opposite the stricken *Sea Uranus*. As we moved through the narrow channel to the open sea, I followed Lucifurr onto the bow and we looked out at the waters foaming in the darkness ahead.

'Hemingway cat?' I said.

Lucifurr held up his right paw.

'Also known as boxing-cat, conch-cat or six-fingered cat. I'm polydactyl, honey, six toes on each front paw. Hemingway liked having polydactyl cats, hence the name.'

'Right.'

'Sailors think we are good luck. Six toes are good for hunting and climbing you see – keeps the ships' rodents down.'

He flashed his six claws out and retracted them as quickly.

'Didn't you ever notice, *detective,*' he miaowed, 'or can't you count?'

'No, I didn't,' I lied, looking at him. I just hadn't wanted to mention it.

He leaned in and nuzzled my head. This was unexpected.

'Thanks,' he miaow-whispered.

'Err, OK,' I said, thinking that was quite enough of that.

We sat in awkward silence beside each other in the gap behind the bow sprit, peering over the forward gunnel as the whelker was steered forward to break through the waves.

Spray lashed in an arc over us onto the deck behind, but we were already soaked from the ever-thickening rain. I glanced back at the lights of the retreating harbour. No turning back now.

'Look,' said Lucifurr. 'The wind farm.'

I turned to look ahead. Through the storm, I could just see the flashing red lights on top of the turbine hubs. The whelker's storm jib had been unfurled and was helping to keep the ship steady, but we were still being buffeted heavily by every swell, so it was difficult to keep our destination in view.

'Which turbine is it?' shouted Anny behind us.

'The one that looks slightly different, keep an eye on out,' Rack shouted back.

All the turbines' blades still seemed to be turning, though I knew they would be stopped automatically once the wind speeds exceeded a certain point. Minutes passed as the *Perky Pecker* crashed through wave after wave, edging ever closer to the edge of the wind farm. The boat was like a miniscule swimmer, crawling over each slope of water then rolling down behind the passing wave before beginning another painful slow ascent. Then at last we were in the middle of the wind farm, watching the waves crashing around the turbines' bright yellow lower sections, the transition pieces.

'There! That one!' shouted Mary, who was at the tiller.

We followed the direction of her pointing finger. To our left, on the perimeter of the wind farm facing the Whitstable shoreline, one of the turbines had stopped its blades turning and was slowly opening the nacelle doors above its hub. It was as if a giant were neatly splitting apart its skull to expose his brain to the elements.

'Bear to port!' shouted Rack.

Slowly and painfully the *Perky Pecker* battled its way to the bright yellow steel transition piece supporting the turbine tower looming above us. Bolted to it was a metal ladder leading to a platform high above the waves. On that platform would be the entrance to the interior of the turbine. But there was no way any of us could climb the ladder with the waves sweeping like haymaking blows across its rungs. We were momentarily stumped, until Rack pointed at a small horizontal ramp a third of the way up the ladder. He shouted to Mary above the roar of the water.

'That's the splash line ramp. Get us close and we'll jump across.'

Mary edged the *Perky Pecker* as close as possible to the tiny, railed platform. The storm surge tide had raised the water level close to it. With each passing wave the boat rose momentarily so high that the bow was level with it. Rack and Anny came forward and prepared themselves to leap across.

'Come on,' said Lucifurr. 'This is where we get off.'

I don't know how the four of us made it across the rising and crashing seas that boiled around the tiny whelker. We timed our leap to take advantage of a particularly large wave which lifted the tiny boat up above the level of the ramp. Lucifurr and I flew above the churning spray and landed in a messy bundle on the hard steel while Anny and Rack grasped the rail they'd both slammed into. Anny saw Rack bounce off it to fall back and pulled him up and over just before he slid down into the retreating water. Lucifurr and I crouched close to the transition piece's wall watching their scrabbling antics. Note to humans, I thought – for jumping safely, four legs good, two legs bad. We all lay in a heap for a silent sodden moment wondering what the hell we'd done, until Anny spoke again.

'The cats have jumped with us,' she said matter-of-factly.

'I noticed,' said Rack, 'they must have thought we were abandoning ship.'

'Nothing for it then,' replied Anny.

'No, best get on,' said Rack.

They stood shakily and picked us up. Anny squeezed me inside the large chest pocket of her storm jacket while Lucifurr draped himself around the neckpiece of Rack's smock, his claws deep in its water-proof material. I could just peer out of the pocket by lying sideways and keeping my paw wedged against the pocket flap. It was like being carried in a litter looking out from inside a post-box.

Rack and Anny climbed the rungs to the platform and opened the steel door to the interior of the turbine tower. Inside, muted lights illuminated the small space, which was crowded with control equipment. We crept in and Anny closed the door gently. We heard the low hum of the generator high above us, muted by the background storm noise outside.

Rack signalled to Anny for us to be silent and pointed across to the small two-person lift in the corner. We squeezed into it and Anny pressed the ascent button. The cable tensed and the lift rose almost silently into space, calmly eating up the distance to the nacelle. Inside, we watched through the safety grille door as the endless smooth grey steel interior of the tower passed us by. Trapped in the tiny rising metal box, we were all crapping ourselves. And nowhere to dig a hole to bury it in either.

The lift came to a gentle stop short of the nacelle where the tower narrowed down close to the top. We stepped out onto a half platform and looked up. We could see the closed hatch to the nacelle. The last few yards' climb were again by steel ladder. Stupidly, I leaned out of Anny's pocket and peered down over the edge of the platform into the abyss below. I felt my legs weaken to wet pouch food. Holy Bastet, that was a long drop.

At that moment, Anny tucked my head back into the smock's pocket and started up the ladder, with Rack sporting his black Lucifurr collar following closely behind. The howling wind and rain in the open nacelle disguised the sound of the hatch being opened. Rack and Anny raised themselves into the nacelle and looked around, buffeted by the furious gusts of wind. Lucifurr leapt down from Rack's neck and disappeared behind the bulky generator that dominated the rear of the tightly packed space now open to the elements. I struggled to get out of the smock pocket, but Anny was holding me in too tightly. I let out a low growl of anger then caught myself.

Then we saw her. Looking out beyond the rotor and blades at the front of the nacelle, a woman in skin-tight waterproofs wearing oversized headphones was standing on top of the large steel box containing the gear mechanism. She had a thick waist security belt tied to a chain securing her to the box and seemed unaware of our presence, gazing out at the sea and the indistinct lights of Whitstable twinkling beyond. She moved her body and limbs to and fro as if in a trance, the red hair blowing wildly around her head charged with a life of its own. Then she stopped moving, sensing our presence, and turned around. She pushed the earphones down around her neck and smiled.

Rack and Anny were transfixed, but I didn't need an introduction. 'Wild Hog' Fenella Kincaid, who now gazed down on us, was the master-criminal who had killed Ben, my human in Stoke Newington, and terrorised my adopted town into cringing fear. Now she was going to drown Whelkville unless we stopped her.

'You need to stop whatever you are doing!' shouted Rack through the roaring wind.

'Doing? I'm only doing a bit of personal DJing, darling,' replied Fenella. 'Would you and your friend care to join me up here?'

'You can't drown the town!' Anny screamed.

That got Fenella's attention. From her waist belt she removed something coiled up tight and let it unfurl down to the floor of the nacelle. I realised in an instant that it was a bullwhip, the essential accoutrement of every self-respecting dominatrix mastermind. I struggled once more to escape from Anny's grip as both she and Rack involuntarily stepped back to the extreme rear of the nacelle.

'Well, you seem to have worked it out somehow so obviously I'll have to kill you now. And it was a bit unwise of you to bring a pet to the party, sweetie, because this will hurt quite a bit,' she said.

As she said it she arched her back and let the bullwhip's full length fall back behind her.

I felt Anny being pulled hard to her right by Rack, into the gap behind the generator. Then the whip crackled in the spot where she'd been standing an instant before. Anny and Rack crouched low as the whip continued to flick out viciously over the machinery above them. They looked around but there were no tools or turbine parts at hand they could use to defend themselves. Fenella was now laughing uproariously.

'Come on out, little darlings, or I'll have to come back there with my gun, and it will make a terrible mess,' she shouted.

The storm seemed to have reached new heights and the

wind was catching the doors of the open nacelle like steel sails and swaying the entire turbine.

Rack turned to Anny.

'It's no good. I don't think she has a gun. I'll try to rush her and stop her setting off the explosives,' he said.

'Don't be stupid, she's a psychopath,' replied Anny.

'No, it's OK, the whip can't get through these waterproofs,' said Rack.

He took a breath and darted out of our hiding place into the corridor of the nacelle. Then I heard the bullwhip crack, followed by a shout of pain and the sound of something heavy falling to the floor. The whip flicked out again and again, each time followed by dull groans.

Anny screamed and stood up. I took the opportunity to at last scramble out of her smock pocket and jump onto the top of the generator. I had to crouch down to stop the wind carrying me off.

'Stop it! Leave him be!' Anny screamed, running towards Rack's prone figure lying on the steel floor.

Fenella Kincaid had released herself from her safety chain and now stood on the nacelle deck. She lowered her whip and the small pearl-handled revolver she was holding in her other hand. She smiled as Anny kneeled beside her partner and glanced at me.

'Just stay there and don't move an inch, honey,' she shouted, 'this will all soon be over.'

'Why are you doing this?' said Anny, almost to herself.

Kincaid laughed.

'Well darling, since you're not going anywhere I'll let you in on my little secret. After I flood the town, I'll hand myself in to the police in another case. My lawyers tell me the evidence is purely circumstantial and I'm likely to get off or at worst just serve a couple of years.'

I realised in that instant she was referring to being a prime suspect in the murder of councillor Kelda Quick. She was right that the evidence for the murder of the councillor and the Seaview Hill allotments chairperson Broderic Brassica was largely circumstantial. I was pawing myself for not emailing my video evidence to the police – at the time it had seemed superfluous. But why flood the town?

'So I've been scaring the town shitless, driving down property prices and buying up everything I can get my hands on as all the DFLs and the property developers sell up cheap and scarper. All done through shell companies in offshore havens, of course. When I get out of the slammer I'll own most of the Whitstable waterfront. Or as someone might once have said, *après le deluge, c'est moi.*'

'But how did you organise all those outrages on your own? The Two-Tone Tankerton Terror, the Seasalter Staycation Shitshow and the *Sea Uranus* Sinking? Not to mention all the other stuff, the lipped-up lipsticks, the tipped-over terracotta pots and the wayward wheelie bins?' said Anny.

'Easy,' Fenella replied. 'After the Winkle Iron Footbridge debacle I told the disgraced leadership of the Preservation Alliance of Whitstable I could return the town to the 1950s if they agreed to help. The PAW fell over themselves to carry out their "direct preservation action".'

Kincaid glanced at her watch and back at Anny.

'It's 3am, darling. The storm surge should be at its strongest and I've got another little job to do first. Don't move an inch till I come back – I won't hesitate to use this,' she said, raising her pistol.

Without another word she strode to the front of the nacelle, re-coiling her bullwhip and holstering her pistol. She stood by the bearings covering the main rotor shaft and knelt to look at the data on the rugged laptop she had left on the floor. She glanced at a wired mechanism beside it, which I took to be the explosive primer. Then she stood and tried to lean over the rotor hub to look down at the foaming sea. Perhaps she wanted to make sure the waves were really at their height. In another moment she might spot Mary struggling to keep the *Perky Pecker* in position at the base of the turbine. But the view was clearly obstructed.

So I prayed for her to do what she did next.

Kincaid swore and looked at the two open concave doors of the nacelle, spanning its length. If she climbed on the nearest of them, she could stand or kneel on that part closest to the hydraulic hinges, which was nearly horizontal, and grip the front edge of the door to look down. She glanced back at Anny comforting Rack and tapped her pistol. Then she lifted herself onto the nacelle door and crawled forward on her hands and knees to protect herself from the wind until she reached the edge. She looked down at the base of the turbine three hundred feet below. I heard her exclaim something in anger and just thought, now, Lucifurr, now.

He came like a demon, leaping over the rotor shaft between the gearbox and the generator and up onto the nacelle door in an instant. She must have sensed something behind her, as she started to turn around and reach for her gun, but it was too late. Lucifurr plunged his teeth through her skin-tight waterproofs into her protruding arse before she could defend herself. Her face registered the surprise for just a moment before she howled out like some banshee spirit.

Anny turned around and stood up. I'd already leapt from the gearbox and was sprinting along the gangway. I felt it vibrate as Anny started to run behind me.

Ahead, there was an almighty thrashing about on the nacelle door as Kincaid used all her burlesque, pole dancing and general booty-shaking experience to try to dislodge Lucifurr's fangs from her no doubt heavily injected glutes.

Then she made her last mistake, lifting her hands from their grip on the edge of the nacelle door to flap behind her at Lucifurr, as if she was wafting away the stink of a particularly eggy one. A sudden sharp gust from behind caught her and instantly she was tipping over, screaming out, her hands trying to grip something, anything to steady herself. Unfortunately, the only thing her left hand gripped for an instant was Lucifurr, just as he'd released his toothy grip from her bum. For once his balance failed him and he followed her over, twisting and turning back in the wind. I reached him as he stretched out agonisingly for the edge of the nacelle door and shot out my own paw. But he was just too far out.

I yowled out his name as he started to fall away, looking up at me. Did he smile for a moment?

I leaned out further, then felt hands around my body, pulling me away. I fought and scratched and twisted but to no avail. Anny pulled me close to her chest.

'I'm sorry, darling, he's gone,' she said softly.

And then I really yowled.

I don't remember the ride back down in that sardine-can lift with Anny to the *Perky Pecker*. It was an hour later and the storm had temporarily subsided, but was expected to pick up again later. Anny had closed the nacelle doors, found the first aid kit and patched Rack up after phoning the police. First-aid and bomb-disposal experts were on their way on the RNLI boat and she'd been told to leave Rack in the nacelle until they arrived and get herself and Mary back to Whitstable as soon as possible.

The sea was much calmer as we transferred to the *Perky Pecker*. Mary was at the tiller and waved cheerfully at us as we came aboard. I was back in Anny's smock chest pocket and looked at our intrepid pilot. Why was she smiling so broadly?

'He's up near the bow – I've made him a bed while he recovers,' she said.

I wrestled furiously out of the smock pocket while both women laughed. I leapt down onto the deck and raced across it and there he was, lying asleep on a blanket inside a curled rope. As I miaowed on approach, he opened his eyes a smidgeon. I screeched to a halt next to his improvised cat basket. 'How? What? How have you survived?' I said breathlessly.

'Missed me?' Lucifurr said quietly. 'I told you I was descended from Unsinkable Sam.'

He closed his eyes again and I leaned forward to nuzzle his side. Mary was talking behind me.

'I only found him quarter of an hour ago. I think he came down in the storm jib, which I'd loosened when the gusts really got scary. The *Perky Pecker* was heeling too much and I just couldn't keep her close to the turbine. She was still heeling after I did it though and I suppose the jib just scooped him up when he fell. He's pretty bruised though.'

'What about Fenella Kincaid?' said Anny.

'Oh, she made the ship as well,' said Mary, pointing up,

'that's why they want us to get to port asap.'

We followed her gaze upward. At the top, arms and legs spreadeagled and neatly impaled on the main mast, her red hair flowing around her ashen face in the light breeze, was 'Wild Hog' Fenella Kincaid, would-be Whitstable property monopolist. The mast swayed to and fro in a sad waltz as the ship moved in the churning sea.

The perfect end for that particular pole dancer, I said to myself.

🐾

'I've entered you for my *Felinness Book of Records*,' said Ross. 'Longest cat dive at sea – 105 metres.'

'Thanks,' said Lucifurr, sounding distinctly uninterested.

It was a week later and we were meeting up after Lucifurr's vet stay and enforced home recovery. 'The Cat who Saved Whitstable', as the papers had dubbed him, was now hot property and the film and advert offers were flooding in to his owners.

'I'll have to run away and find new humans if this goes on,' he'd muttered when he'd finally emerged from his convalescence.

'I expect it'll all calm down as soon as there's a new crime story in the local press,' I said.

'You know what saved you? Pure instinct and simple physics,' said Ross.

'Explain,' I said.

'Well, when we fall we straighten ourselves to land, and once we reach terminal velocity of 60 mph we relax and our legs splay out like a flying squirrel. So we maximise our wind resistance. Normally, if a cat hits the ground like that she or he can break ribs but still survive. But you fell into a sail as soft as a hammock, you lucky so and so,' said Ross.

'What about Fenella – would she have survived if she'd hit the jib sail?' I asked.

'Nah, her terminal velocity would have been 120 mph. She'd have ripped through it like a cannonball. Plus humans have no righting reflex, they just do a lot of screaming and flapping about.'

'Still,' I said, 'dive fast, die young, leave a skewered-looking corpse.'

'That's cold,' said Lucifurr, winking at me.

I'd managed to conceal my role in saving Whelkville by making myself scarce as soon as I'd leapt ashore in Whitstable Harbour. Anny and Mary had rushed Lucifurr to the vets and I'd slipped into the untidy pile of lobster pots at the quayside, where Ross was still waiting. I'd miaowed softly with mirth at his worried expression and we'd headed home side by side in silence. I'd slept the sleep of the dead that night, dreaming of sitting on Ben's lap in our old Stokie flat telling him how I'd put things right as far as his killers were concerned. He'd smiled, stroking my ears and back until I'd nodded off.

I awoke late, totally happy, to one of those fresh autumn days where it feels as if the world has been washed clean.

It never is.

Postscript – In Cat We Trust

WHELKVILLE IS STILL A MYSTERY TO ME, BUT IT HAS GOT under my skin.

I once promised myself I'd leave Grace as soon as I'd cleaned up the town and revenged myself on the Kincaids. Many cats do leave their humans once they find a better option. But I think I'll hang around a bit. Grace would be lost without me around the place, and she always calls out for me and Ross as soon as she comes in after another hard shift saving lives in the Covid ward. She thinks we're hers and Jane's kids, the sad deluded cow. In reality, we look after them. And help Jane and her sidekick Alf clean up the dirty corners of this criminal sinkhole, of course.

That evening, I went back up to the spare bedroom and jumped on the sofa to look out at another blazing red sunset over the town. The case had been disturbing for me, and I mused over it as I surveyed the tiny houses and bungalows illuminated by the evening hues. I had become too human in it, and stopped being myself. What was I thinking, trying to apply rationality to the economic crisis Fenella had created in order to solve Whitstable's social problems? Buying into all that bogus human certainty, lack of humility and delusions of progress? Christ, that was biped business – I was a *cat*.

I recalled the sad wellness delusions of Selma Dudds in the Kentuka honey case and the cynical use of Situationist philosophy by the Kincaids in their crimes against local art. No wonder our feline space travellers in the Limbless Catalytic case had concluded humans are way short of joining the civilised galaxy. All that theorising bollocks they do to give meaning to their random lives. Why can't they just *be?* Sleep, wake, eat and distract yourself somehow if you feel like it. Humans think we have no capacity to reflect or feel. How would the stupid sods know? What they suffer from is the inability to stop overthinking. And yes, I *felt* Ben's death as keenly as Grace did.

At least some of the criminals we'd caught were just bloody greedy, including Fenella Kincaid. There is some twisted honesty in that.

Well, I still wanted to distract myself with more than a ball of string or a cat-nip infused bug toy. So I gazed down on Whelkville and decided there was still life left for me in this criminal playground.

Just try to stop me.

Printed in Great Britain
by Amazon